SO PROUDLY THEY HAILED

BOOK ONE

OTHER BOOKS BY GAIL HUNTLEY

Blunt Force Winds

Conquering the Wild

Long Lake, Adirondack Heartland

REVIEWS FROM AMAZON.COM

Reviews from *Long Lake, Adirondack Heartland*

"Wonderful book full of great stories, pictures and information! We had gone camping on Long Lake and wanted to know about the storms, the camps, and the other history. This had it!"

"Really enjoyed the details of the area and the 'homespun' tales of the families that live(d) there."

Conquering the Wild

"I totally enjoyed reading this book. Having ancestors who were some of the first settlers in Long Lake, Abram Rice was my Great, Great Grandfather, I was especially excited to read it. I loved the way the book was written in chronological order of the families who settled there. Having a love for Long Lake I could visualize the settlers traveling the trails and paddling the lake. I think anyone who has a love for Long Lake or the history of the Adirondacks would love this book. I look forward to Book #2 with the continuation of the history of Long Lake!"

Blunt Force Winds

"Not only was this a book about the inspiring author Gail Huntley, it kept me on the edge of my seat. During the reading of this book I felt sad, joyous, angry, and hopeful. This author brings about feelings in the reader. Great read!"

SO PROUDLY
THEY HAILED

BOOK ONE

BY

GAIL HUNTLEY

www.bookstandpublishing.com

Published by
Bookstand Publishing
Morgan Hill, CA 95037
4612_3

Cover photo: Lou Plumley,
descendant of first settler in Long Lake,
Joel Plumley.

ISBN 978-1-63498-666-3

Printed in the United States of America

DEDICATED TO

Uncle Roger and Aunt Ann Latimer Huntley

ACKNOWLEDGEMENTS

Many years ago, my father handed me a book written by George Dalzell, my ancestor whose parents were Charles and Annie Dodds Dalzell. His grandparents were born in Scotland and England, respectively. He spent his boyhood in Waddington, New York and later became Secretary to the Committee on Admissions and Grievances of the District of Columbia; he spent much of his retirement researching British and Scottish history. I remember him typing on the old black typewriter at my grandfather's farmhouse in Crary Mills, New York. He was a maritime lawyer and the book documented the life of the Doddses' family in Scotland, their journey to America, and their life upon settling down. My grandmother was Annie Dodds Huntley and "So Proudly They Hail," is based on the true story of her lineage from both sides; her paternal side from Lessudden, Scotland and her maternal side from Jedburgh, Scotland. I am deeply grateful to this man for writing this journal, "Immigration of the Dodds Family to America." I also want to thank my father, Howard Huntley for preserving the journal, and instilling in me a love of history. Thanks to my brother, Larry, for making copies of the book for me.

I am also amazed and deeply thankful to my Aunt Ann Huntley for collecting newspaper articles, letters, and pictures of the Doddses,

Rules, Waltons, and Huntley families, and sharing this valuable history with me. I am so appreciative of the time my Aunt Ann, and sister, Venita, spent with me in Waddington, New York researching our ancestry.

Thank you to Martha Francis, my editor, for all her suggestions and challenging work. To Andy Baldwin of Bookstand Publishing for continuing to advise me throughout the publication process. Much gratitude to Joan Burke, Director of the Newcomb Historical Museum, for her help and Laurinda Minke for sending me the wonderful map. Thank you Donna Lagoy, historian, of Chestertown, New York, for the valuable information and answers to my questions.

TABLE OF CONTENTS

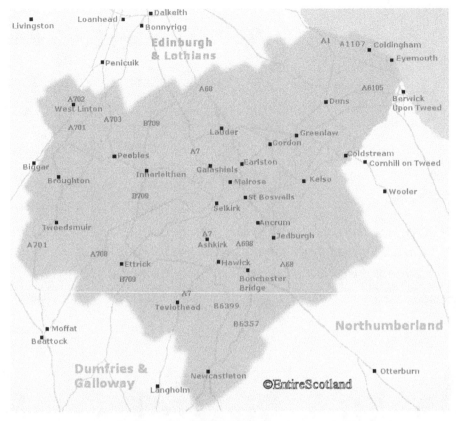

Figure 1. Lessudden, home of Thomas and Helen Dodds, was changed to St Boswell.

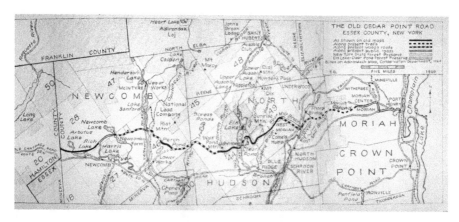

Figure 2. Journey of Jenny Dodds Walton from Crown Point on the Carthage Road to Newcomb on the Cedar Point Road, 1800s. From the collection of the Newcomb Historical Museum.

CHAPTER I

1816

The village of Lessudden, Scotland, was a group of simple stone buildings aligned along the curve of a broad street. Beginning on the north side of town, a short stroll brought you to the Brae Heads (hilltops), from which you could view the River Tweed. A deep pool overhung by white birches and the green-leafed alders hid young lovers who carved their initials in the black bark. The breadth of the Tweed was that of a wide creek, and in the bottomland was Dryburgh Abbey. The decaying abbey had housed monks at one time and included a tower you could see for miles. Bordering the abbey was the Coulter farm, and day by day ten-year-old Robert Dodds watched as the new tower rose up next to the Coulter barn. Local stonemasons placed stone after stone strategically in round rows moving upward already past the height of the barn roof. No other owner in the area had one of these structures. Robert asked his da what it was, and Thomas told him it was a silo, constructed to hold feed for cows. Most farms stored their animal feed underground, not above, but now several European countries were adding these towers to their barns.

Though warned by his father to stay away from the construction, Robert could not contain his curiosity and began sneaking down the glen and looking at the silo. Upon close examination of this giant cone, Robert discovered little handles embedded in the stone. They went straight up to a little door at the top of the structure. He put his hand on the highest rung he could reach, stepped onto the one next to the ground, and pulled himself up. "Hey, Laddie!" Cyrus Coulter bellowed. Robert quickly jumped to the ground. "Well if it isn't Robert Dodds. Now, you get out a here and stay off my silo!"

"Uh … uh. I am sorry." Robert made a circle in the dirt with his foot praying to be anywhere but standing in front of angry Laird Coulter.

"Well, off you go then, Lad. Off you go. I catch you down here again, Laddie, and I'll be telling your da." He waved his hand and shook his head as he watched young Robert run up the hill. Laird Coulter hoped he scared the boy enough to keep him from climbing, but he knew those brackets made it too tempting for a young lad or lassie to resist. He would have to keep an eye out. Within a few weeks, young Robert had forgotten the incident.

One morning, when the sun tore through the crisp spring air, Robert woke up knowing that today would be the day that he would climb that tower. It was plowing season, so the workers would be out in the field. He jumped out of bed, snuck out the door, and tore down to that silo. He knew that his sister, Ann, was already at the Bryden farm shearing sheep, and Jenny was babysitting for Lady Rutherford. Da was hard at work in town replacing a door at the local pub, and Ma was in the house. Climbing was Robert's favorite hobby, and he was good at it. He had climbed every door, every wall, every alder and birch tree within five miles, and he had touched every thatched roof in the valley, but he had never climbed a silo. He arrived around 10:00 AM, and as he predicted, no one was around. Many times, Robert had ventured off to nearby Drysdale Abbey and tried to climb the few standing walls, but there were no footholds. He had also investigated the tower just a couple miles north of the Tweed, but the smooth tower walls were unclimbable.

It was an unusually clear morning, so as Robert scaled the silo, he could see the green hills blanketed with buds of heather ready to pop and shower the glen in purple splendor. Even Scottish children appreciated the beauty of the hills and the heather. Soon he was high enough to see the thatched roof of the little cottage where he was born. Black-faced sheep dotted the countryside like hundreds of woolen balls scattered over the hills. Robert took another step with his right foot, but when he stood up on the handle, it broke, and his foot slipped off, leaving him dangling halfway up the tower. He barely had a grasp on the handle above him with his right hand. A scream ripped through his head, and he began to panic. He thought, 'I must hold on, get my footing on something, and grab hold with my other hand.' He took a breath, put his toes hard against the rough stone of the tower, and managed to pull himself up enough to grab the bar with his other hand. He had it now, but he soon discovered that the bar below his feet was too far down to touch; so now he was dangling with no way down.

Robert began to scream, "Help! Somebody help me!" He screamed until his voice was raw. He screamed until his screams turned to cries, and his cries turned to groans, as stabbing pain tore through his shoulder sockets. He tried climbing up the wall with his feet to give his shoulders relief, but it did not help. He frantically searched for a way out. Was there a chance that if he let go, he could drop down and grab onto the bar that was six feet below him, or would he be going too fast to do that? He scoured the countryside in front of him. Maybe Da would be coming home or his sister, Jenny, would be finished babysitting.

He could see the tower behind Walter Scott's manor. Oh, why couldn't Mr. Scott or his nephew, John, come riding down that hill right now like they did every morning? Oh, what he would give to even see Laird Coulter right now. As he gazed over the green hills and the rooftops of the houses in Lessudden, he wondered how his ma and da would handle their second son dying. They had already lost one. Before Jenny was born, they had a son who had died at birth. Da said Ma was sad for a long time. He would mostly miss Ann, with her red pigtails flying in the winter wind. She was always happy. Ann had probably already climbed this tower, probably climbed it to the top and back down like she did everything. 'I wonder what it will feel like when I hit the ground.' He had to think about that because he knew his arms would soon give out. Then another idea came to him: before his arms gave out, he should let go and try to grab that bar below him. At least it would be a chance. He said a prayer and asked God to make it not hurt too much when he landed; then he shut his eyes and began to loosen his hold on the bar.

"What are you doing up there, Robert?" Robert heard that familiar voice and, thinking he was dead, opened his eyes, looked down, and saw the red pigtails swaying in the air as his thirteen-year-old sister ran toward him. "Hold on; just hold on, Robert. I'm coming." Ann began climbing the silo.

"Ann, Ann," he whispered, crying, "I can't hold on any longer."

"You will hold on! I'm here. How stupid can you be? I can't believe you did this!" she chided as she hurried up the silo. She heard him whimper and groan and knew he was terrified. She said nothing more, concentrating on getting to him before he fell. Soon she saw the broken handrail and figured out what had happened. She stood on the rung beneath the broken one and shouted up to Robert, "Robert, put your feet on my shoulders!"

"I can't. I can't reach!" he cried.

"Yes, you can. I am right here." She reached up and touched his right leg putting it on one of her shoulders then did the same with his left leg. Immediately, Robert felt his muscles twinge with relief. 'Okay,' Ann, thought; 'now what? How do I get him down?' The broken rail hung to the side, but the left side rivet was still secure. She had an idea. "Robert, I am going to hold your left leg, and I want you to step down onto the broken handle. It is still attached so you must turn your right foot to the side and step onto it. Then I will help you get your left leg down to the handle I am standing on."

"But it is broken!" Robert sputtered between tears.

"It is your only chance. Robert, you must trust me." As far back as Robert could remember, it had been Ann who had checked on him on stormy nights, Ann who watched out for him when he toddled out in the front yard, and Ann who came to him when Da had to punish him. She would not let him fall. Slowly, he lowered his foot down the side of the tower. Ann grabbed his foot and guided it to the spike. Then, she held onto a handle with one hand and grabbed him around the hips. "Now, let go, Robert." He let go, and she slid him against her stomach. "Put your foot on top of mine." He stretched down and found her foot. Ann cringed with pain but did not care. She only cared about getting her brother to safety. Now she had to let go, reach down, grab the bar their feet were on, and inch down so Robert could follow. "Okay, Robert, I am going to pull my foot out. Slide your foot over as far as you can so I can get my fingers around the bar." This was going to be tricky and scary. She held onto the handle above her with her left hand and reached down for the handle she stood on with her right hand. She could not reach it. She tried again and stretched as far as she could to no avail. By now, a morning wind had snarled up. She looked up at the sky and saw the familiar rain clouds coming from the west. Rain would make everything slippery. She had to hurry. She frantically scanned the landscape, hoping for anyone returning from plowing or Da coming home for lunch. There was no one. She could yell; however, yelling this far up would be inaudible in the wind even if someone were around. The only reason she had found Robert was that she was coming back from the Baron Bryden's place. She had not heard her brother screaming. She had seen him. 'Maybe I should have gotten help,' but she had feared that by the time she returned Robert would have fallen. Suddenly, she had an idea. "Robert, can you be really strong and hang onto that bar with both hands and not let go no matter what?"

"I think so, Ann."

"Good, because I am going to let go and wrap my arms around you; you are going to hold us up for just a few minutes while I slide down you and get to the next foot and hand holds."

"What?"

"Just don't let go, Robert. Don't move, okay?"

"Okay." Ann let her left hand go and wrapped it around Robert's waist; then, she released her right hand, grabbed onto his shirt, and slowly lowered herself down until she felt the bar safely under the toe of her shoe. She held onto Robert's legs and slid her left hand onto the bar beside his feet. "Okay, Robert, we are good. I am going down now, and you will follow." She began the descent to the bottom, as did Robert. When they reached the bottom, he fell into her arms and cried shamelessly until there were no more tears.

Ann stood in front of Robert, her eyes inches from his and said forcefully, "You will never do that again, right?"

"No, I never will. I was so scared, Ann. Do you have to tell Da?"

"No, if you promise never to try anything like this again."

"I won't."

"Okay, little one, time for lunch. Let's race home. Last one home does the dishes!" Robert wanted to be the last one home, and he was; he happily washed the dishes for his sister that day.

Gail Huntley

Chapter II

It was the day of the great fair, a celebration centered in Lessudden Square on July 18th, and the whole town was abuzz with the sounds of celebration. Thomas Dodds would be bringing in the prize black-faced sheep and the two horses he raised on the farm. His wife, Helen, was busy cooking and making sure their children, Tom, Jr., Jenny, Robert, Ann, Mary, and George wore their best clothes. This year, as every year, Helen was entering the contest for the prize Scotch steak pie. Their neighbor, Jane Ryan, usually won this contest, but this year Helen was trying a new recipe. She was sure this recipe would win.

Helen was not from Lessudden. She was from Jedburgh, a larger town about eight miles south; it was not unusual for folks from Lessudden to come to the small city for supplies. Helen's parents, John and Agnes Rule owned a general store in Jedburgh where she had worked from early childhood through her teenage years, until she married Thomas. She met Thomas on a spring day when he waltzed into their store with his father. As she kneaded the bread for the fair, she recalled the first time she saw this tall boy with jet-black hair and large brown eyes. He was about sixteen years old and already a head taller than his da. He did the ordering, and she was amazed that he knew the total before she even finished the calculations. He would visit her store several times before he asked, "What is your name?"

She sputtered and stammered and eked out, "Helen, my, my name is Helen Rule." Then she stood there feeling as stupid as one could ever feel.

"Uh, my name is Thomas Dodds," the boy said. She realized that she had not said a word back to him: not asked him his name, not asked him how he was, and not even mentioned the rain coming down.

Finally, she caught her breath and answered, "Hi, Thomas, nice to meet you."

"And also you," the young man said as he took off his cap and bowed his head. He looked at her and smiled, and Helen's heart melted right there in the middle of the store. He had the whitest teeth she had ever seen, gleaming through his sunburnt skin. Helen smiled back and continued the transaction, and then he was out the door. Every day, Helen wished she had said this and wondered why she had not said that. She couldn't wait for him to return. She knew it could be a week, a month, or six months before he came back. It was a year before he returned. She had given up on seeing him again, thinking he must have moved away or something dreadful had happened to him. She had not dared write the address on the invoice, as it was Duke Buccleuch's land the Doddses lived on, and she could not know if the letter would go to his manor or the Doddses' cottage.

When Thomas did return, he came through the door alone. Helen was behind the counter putting cans on the shelf with her back to him. He walked up to the counter and said, "Good Morning, Helen."

She turned and was again rendered speechless. There stood Thomas Dodds, and he remembered her name. 'Where had he been all this time?' she wondered.

"A good morning to you, I said," Thomas repeated.

"Uh, oh, yes, and a good morning; it is Thomas, right?"

"Yes."

Helen placed the can in her hand on the counter and walked over, standing in front of Thomas, "You have not been here in a long time."

"Yes, I know, but not because I did not want to come. Da needed me on the farm when he was gone. I had to come today because he is a joiner and travels quite far these days for work."

"Oh, I am sorry he is away so much."

"Oh, I like it because now I am old enough to do the buying and come here to see you."

Helen smiled, looked down, and felt the heat slowly riding up her neck and into her face. "Oh, uh, well, okay; what can I help you with?" 'God,' she thought, 'why can't I say anything that doesn't sound like I am deranged?'

Tom handed her a list of items and then proposed that she have lunch with him.

"Really, you want to have lunch with me?"

"Really, I want to have lunch with you, Helen Rule." And so began the courtship of Thomas Dodds and Helen Rule. A relationship spanning eight miles was difficult in many ways. If Thomas rode his horse or took a carriage, it took at least an hour out of his day, which he could not spare. Therefore, Helen usually made the trip. She fell in love with Thomas' mother, Mrs. Dodds, and soon the wedding day was planned. Thomas and Helen were married at the local Presbyterian Church in Lessudden, and Helen came to live in the little cottage. It did not compare to what Helen had come from. Her house in Jedburgh had several bedrooms upstairs, a kitchen, a dining room, a sitting room, and an outhouse attached to the porch. The Doddses' place had two bedrooms, and one was the loft.

Helen put the bread in the pans and thought about the first time she had entered this little cottage that was now home to her. Upon entering, the first thing she had seen was the chimney place. It provided the heat and a fire for cooking. Thomas Dodds, Sr., had loaded the stove with faggots and turf. A bucket of salt was kept near the fire to keep dry, because salt was taxed. There was only one window in the cottage since windows were also taxed. Consequently, it stayed quite dark even in the daytime. Several lanterns were placed strategically on small wooden shelves throughout the structure. A chain with hooks hung from inside the fireplace; on one of the hooks was Mrs. Dodds' griddle for scones. The floors were scoured and sanded, and there was a mahogany table flanked by benches in the middle of the room and a wooden armchair placed strategically by the fire for Mr. Dodds, along with a few straight wooden chairs that Thomas had made. There was a built-in bed shielded by a curtain for Mr. and Mrs. Dodds. Thomas and his da had constructed a 'slip room,' partitioned off between the kitchen and the other bedroom, for Thomas and Helen. The day they were married, they served lamb, haggis, and scones, which was a rare treat. The lambs were raised for wool, not food, but this was a special occasion attended by most of the village.

The voice of her mother-in-law interrupted Helen's thoughts as she was finishing up the biscuits, "Helen, do you have the biscuits finished?"

"Oh, come in, Ellen; I'm just starting to wrap them." Helen's mother had taught her weaving, spinning, and cooking, but Ellen Dodds had taught Helen how to make the delicious biscuits she was bringing to the fair. This morning, Ellen had come over to help wrap the biscuits in warm towels to bring to the food table.

"Well, you have most of it finished. Sorry I was a little late. With the fair starting up, Thomas had a couple extra at the jail, and I had to feed them." Thomas Sr. and Ellen Dodds had moved into town because the town had elected Thomas Sr. mayor and custodian of the jail. They lived in a flat above the jail, and Ellen cooked the meals for the few prisoners until Thomas freed them or they were sent on to Edinburgh. Thomas Sr. could no longer do the physical work of the farm; this job provided enough for them to live on and for Thomas to enjoy a few drinks at the local pub with his friends.

"Ann, Robert, come here!" shouted Helen. "I need you to carry some of these things to the wagon." No one came. 'Now, where are those two?' she thought as she picked up baby George and put his vest on before placing him in the wagon. Soon she saw the two children rounding the corner; Robert was as dirty as a pig in mud, and Ann's hair was flying around her head as if it had not been tightly braided only an hour before. "Robert, go in and get cleaned up. We must go."

"But, Ma, do we have to go with you? Can Ann and I go by ourselves?"

"I guess so, but not until you have cleaned up. In the meantime, Ann, I need to fix your hair, and then you can help your sister load up the wagon." With many groans and sighs from Ann, Helen finished redoing her braids; soon Ann and Jenny were piling out the door with their arms loaded down with baskets. Thomas waved from the field as he walked behind the sheep he was bringing to the fair. Wright Bryden followed him with his horses and the Laird Richard Rutherford and his son, Jeff, with his cows. The Rutherfords were a proud clan, and Richard was the type to pitch in and do the work himself; however, it was rumored that he could no longer afford workers to run the farm, so he had to do some of it himself. Regardless, Richard was a fine chap, and the other tenant farmers liked him and knew him well.

"Now where is Robert?" Thomas sighed, looking around, "I need him, and he has run off." He shouted up to Helen, "Have you seen Robert?"

"I sent him in to clean up," Helen shouted back.

"Never you mind that; I need him now."

"I'll come, Da," Ann shouted, dropping her basket on the ground and running down the hill, reaching her father in flash. Helen opened her mouth to object but decided it wasn't worth the energy. Ann would always choose men's work and shun women's work. She would have to learn her duties as a woman, but today was not the day. Soon the wagon was loaded, and they began the trek to the square. Robert came down and joined the men. "Nice of you to come by, Robert," Da said. He kept pace with his oldest brother, Tom, Jr.

"Sorry, Da, Ma made me wash up."

"Well, move along now. We got no time to spare." They could already hear the bleat of the bagpipes and smell the delicious aroma of fresh popped corn and haggis. Robert could not wait to get there to play the games, ride the roundabout, and eat the gingerbread men the gypsies made. Several times, they had to slow up for other farmers and gypsies driving their cattle, horses, and wagons to the fair. Several times those wagons got stuck in the mud, but eventually they all made it to the event.

Halfway down the path to the fairgrounds, Helen realized that Jenny was not with them. She looked over at Ellen, "Did you see Jenny?"

"No, the last I saw she was loading up the wagon."

"That girl. I don't know what has gotten into her, but she seems to come up missing regularly. Now I don't have her to help us unload."

"Oh, well, they all get a little scattered during fair day. We can handle it, dear," Ellen soothed as she touched Helen's arm.

"I suppose. I suppose, but I still sometimes wonder about that girl." Helen sighed.

There was no need to wonder where Robert would be on fair day because as soon as Da released him from work, he would run straight to the gypsy wagons. The gypsies were so colorful with their scarlet and bright green colored clothes and paper flowers. There were strange bottles of smelly medicine and many sweets. He ran from wagon to wagon looking for his friend. She was ten years old and traveled all over; Robert thought she had the greatest life ever. Stopping at the first wagon, he asked, "Where is Teresa?"

"Teresa, Teresa, we have lots of Teresas," a toothless woman wearing a purple headscarf cackled. "How about you buy one of my biscuits, and I'll tell you what you want to know."

"No, I can't. Teresa is ten. Her ma is Marie."

"Well, why didn't you say so?" The old woman turned and pointed down the line of wagons. "She is in the third wagon."

"Thank you!" Robert shouted as he began running to the third wagon. He approached the wagon and saw Teresa's aunt arranging items in the back of the wagon. She was wearing a dark purple skirt and white blouse that showed a lot of chest. As young as he was, Robert's heart skipped a beat when he saw her.

"My, my, Robert, you have grown much from last year."

"Uh, yes, Ma'am." He put his head down. She was so pretty with her long black hair cascading over her shoulders. Robert did not think he had ever seen a prettier lady. Marie came out of the wagon and smiled at Robert.

"Ma'am? No Ma'am. You remember? You call me Sarah or Aunt Sarah."

"Yes, ma…. Sarah." Robert shuffled his feet and waited for what seemed like an eternity.

"Teresa, look who is here!" shouted Marie..

Teresa ran out from behind the wagon. "Robert, I wondered when you would get here. I've been waiting."

"Had to help Da, but can you go now?"

"Ma?"

"Oh, yes, yes, off you two go. Here, Teresa, money for the games." She handed Teresa several coins.

"Thank you, Ma." She hugged her, and they ran off toward the center of the greens, Robert glancing back one last time at Teresa's aunt. She smiled at him, knowing the thoughts and feelings that go through a young boy's head and heart upon seeing a beautiful woman. She liked this boy and thought he would be good for her niece though they could not marry because a gypsy marries a gypsy.

Soon Robert and Teresa were riding the hobbyhorses, trying to knock the coconut shies off their settings, and testing their luck at the shooting gallery. Robert won a small ceramic roan and gave it to Teresa.

When they rounded the corner to enter the gates to the animal cages, Robert stopped dead in his tracks. Standing in front of a man who was leaning against the post office wall was his sister, Jenny. "Teresa, stop for a minute." Robert backed up and stared at the two figures; this was his sister, but he could not see the man. Just as he was about to inch closer, they turned and walked around the corner of the building.

"So, what are we doing? Why are we stopped?" Teresa asked.

"Uh, did you see that girl and boy down by the post office?"

"Yes, so what?"

17

"That was my sister."

"Ok, and so what?"

"Well, I think she was kissing a boy a minute ago." Teresa could have just kept saying "so what" because that did not seem unusual to her. They were young people kissing. Gypsies usually dated young and married young. Displays of affection were seen regularly.

"Uh, huh, come on Robert, let's get a gingerbread."

He looked over once again at the space where he had seen his sister; he wanted to follow them, but the delicious smell of gingerbread biscuits won him over, and he dashed off with Teresa in pursuit of the prize item at the fair.

While Robert was jamming gingerbreads in his mouth, Jenny Dodds and John Scott were walking arm and arm down the footpath out of town into the wild pansies, through the eyebrights, and right into the path of his uncle, Walter Scott. John pushed Jenny into the bushes hoping that his uncle had not seen them.

Walter was riding his favorite horse to the fair and had decided to take the path that had not been used in many years, or so he thought. As Walter approached the bushes, John and Jenny held their breath. They watched Uncle Walter pass them. Jenny sighed in relief. They peered through the open slits between the thistle leaves watching for him to round the bend, so they could come out.

"You might as well come out of there, Lad and Lassie. I saw you way back away," he said as he reined in his horse, backed up, and peered into their bush. "Come on. Come on out you two." Reluctantly,

John came out from behind the bush, and Jenny followed. "And what might you be doing down this hidden path with Jenny Dodds, Lad?"

"We were just coming back home. Uh, it is not what you think."

"And what might I think?"

"Uh, that, that…."

"That you were taking a lady down the path to sneak a wee kiss?"

"Uh, no, no. We are friends."

"Oh, yes, I see. Well, since you are only friends, I guess I might mention what I saw to your da?"

"Uncle, no."

"Please Mister Scott, don't do that."

"Friends, huh. That is what I thought. All I can say is may the Lord be with you when your parents find out." With that, he shook the reins and continued his journey to the fair.

"Oh, John, will he tell?"

"He didn't say he would."

"And he didn't say he would not. John, we must not see each other again."

"I know; I know, Jen."

She looked up at him and whispered, "But we won't stop, will we?"

"No, oh no, Jen," he said knowing he was unable to stop the desire that rose up in him whenever he was close to her.

"We will, John; just not today," Jenny whispered as John pulled away, staring deep into her soft brown eyes, losing all sense of sound, thought, and smell.

"No, my love, not today." He encircled her in his arms, pulled her to him, and kissed her hard and long as they stood in the middle of the path, in the middle of the day where only passion was present.

CHAPTER III

As morning broke, Thomas Dodds stood at the door of the tiny stone cottage nestled beneath the three peaks of Eildon Hills, Scotland. The morning mists lay low after the night rain had turned the River Tweed into an avalanche of rolling waves. Thomas had his own battles to fight, keeping up the farm he was hired to run, taking care of his family, and tending to his carpentry customers. He was the wheelwright of Lessudden, scraping out a living fixing wagon wheels and building gates, boxes, shutters, sheds, and coffins. He was also a master carpenter, and his chest of joiner's tools was among his most cherished possessions. Thomas rented this sheep farm from Duke Henry Scott, the Third Duke of Buccleuch.

Looking out over the shrouded hills, Thomas noticed a person running across the meadow. He squinted his eyes but could not make out who it was until he heard the high-pitched yell of his daughter Ann. He began running toward her, fearing that she was in trouble. She had left to do her morning chores for the Baron Bryden, but she should not be finished this early.

"Da," Ann shouted as she came out of the haze, her long wool scarf trailing behind her. She looked like a ghost floating above the rocky pasture.

"Ann, what is it? Are you hurt?"

Ann reached Thomas and gasped, "It's the sheep, Da; they got the pox."

"What?"

"They are sick, Da, very sick. Mr. Bryden is coming too." Thomas put his arm around Ann's shoulder and looked straight ahead watching Wright Bryden trudge up the hill, his body bent over as if he was hauling a large load behind him. He wore his blue tartan tam he had worn almost every day Thomas had known him. They grew up here in Lessudden. They both had allegiance to the Duke of Buccleuch, and they both were considered a lowland race entitled to no tartan of their own. However, Wright's father, Henry, was from the highlands and though he was born in Lessudden, he honored his highland clan. Henry and Wright had not spoken since Wright joined the military instead of taking over control of the land. After his military stint, Wright set up an ammunition shop in Lessudden. Unfortunately, when the wars ended, his business began to fail. Thomas recalled that it was during this time that Henry Bryden became sick. He died before Wright made it out to the manor. It left a heaviness in Wright that was etched in the lines of his face. Being the oldest son, he had inherited the title and the farm. Reluctantly, he moved in and began to take control, soon discovering that he loved this land. Hence, he worked hard and continually added to the land and the farm. Thomas admired Wright Bryden and knew his father would have been proud of him.

"Morning to you, Wright. Is it true?"

"Think so, Thomas. Are yours sick?"

"No, don't believe so." Ann had last tended their sheep the night before. "Ann?"

"No, not ours, Da."

'Not ours yet,' thought Thomas, as a sickening fear ripped through him. He knew that should this happen to their sheep, the family could not survive. Since the War of 1812 had ended, work had also ended. People no longer needed as many wagons, horseshoes, bridles, or weapons. The shops in the little towns had withered up and closed their doors. Helen Dodds could no longer earn money for sewing uniforms, and as the soldiers went home, farmers such as Thomas were not needed to grow the enormous numbers of crops to feed the soldiers. Now this. If the sheep were to die, he would be blamed and fired, and they would be forced to leave.

"Well, I thought maybe you could have a look, Thomas, before I message the Laird. Ann, you are finished for today. Come back tomorrow."

"Okay, Baron." Ann ran into the house as Thomas and eleven-year-old Tom Jr., and Wright began their trek down the hill and over the bridge to check on the sheep. Tom Jr. worked alongside his da a few days a week before and after school.

Upon reaching the sheep pasture, Thomas pulled his gloves out of his pocket and put them on. Most of the sheep were lying on the ground, while the few standing sheep bleated and trembled as if in pain. 'My God,' Thomas thought, 'most of them are dead.' He bent over and felt the artery in the neck of one of the sheep. He sucked in a sigh of relief. The animal was alive! He noticed that large sores protruded from the lips of the suffering animal. Thomas froze. It was as if someone had hit him hard in the stomach. It was the pox! Ann was right. This disease was highly contagious and could kill a whole herd and neighboring herds of any type of animal. As he walked around looking at the herd, one fact struck him; none of them was dead. "When did you first notice it, Wright?"

"Ann noticed that those two were a little sick last week. I checked them, and they had watery eyes and runny noses but later seemed fine. I kept them in the barn for a few nights, but when Ann let them out this morning she noticed they were not too steady on their feet, and then the others began to get sick."

"Strange that they are still alive. Pox usually kills within days." He looked out over the herd shaking his head then looked down and noticed several clumps of fur stuck to the wet ground. He picked up a clump, examining it, and then looked straight at Wright. "You see any more of this?"

"Yup, they been dropping fur more than usual." With that news, Thomas began looking at the animals' wool coats. Sure enough; there were near bald spots on several of the sick sheep.

"Hmmm; Wright, I don't think it's pox, I think it is flystrike. We have had a lot of rain this last month, and that can do it."

"Uh huh; you know, Thomas, you could be right. Remember when our fathers' sheep got flystrike when we were kids? But what about the mouth sores? They don't go with flystrike."

"Wright, I have seen the sores come when they get this disease; not always but sometimes. Did you tell anyone?"

"Why, no, not yet."

"Don't then. Sheer them. I know it's a bit early, but if you don't you will lose most of their fur. See, it is rotting underneath from the rain." Thomas lifted up the outer layer of wool, so Wright could see the problem. "Wright, we'll help you. I'll get Ann, Helen, and Robert. We'll keep this among ourselves."

The sheep did recover, but Thomas did not. He could not stop thinking about the pending disaster that loomed before his family should one thing go wrong. He was living on a precipice, and at any moment they could fall off the edge. That evening, Thomas asked Helen where the last letter was from her uncle. He opened the letter. It was from America, and Uncle Wright Rule painted a much brighter picture than Thomas was facing here in Scotland. He knew America was a faraway dream. He knew this bright picture of another land was from an uncle who was known through the whole border country of Scotland as a thief. Fifty years ago, border thieves were still common between England and Scotland, and in his day Wright Rule had been one of the best or worst, whichever way you looked at it. After the law began to interfere in the business, thievery was no longer profitable; therefore, before being jailed, Thomas Rule had set sail for the 'promised land.'

That night, as the family gathered around the table, Thomas said the blessing, offering thanks and asking for guidance. Four-year-old Mary began her usual tirade of questions for her da. "When can I go to work? Aren't I big enough to help Ann with the sheep?" Thomas ruffled her dark hair and promised to take her fishing on the Sabbath. That at once quieted her, and she began to eat the meat pie placed before her. Robert, seated next to Tom Jr., could fix a wagon wheel almost as quickly as his father could. He had an aptitude for learning and was already in high school though only ten years old. All the children started school as soon as they could walk. Though the Doddses were tenant farmers, they believed strongly in a good education and strict attendance at the Presbyterian church. Even little George, barely two years, old attended church and would begin school next year while sixteen-year-old Janet, nicknamed Jenny, taught at his school.

Ann looked up at Jenny and asked, "Ah, Jen, how did your chores at the Scotts go today? Did you see Walter Scott?"

"It went fine, Ann. Mr. Scott left early this morning."

Walter Scott had grown up on SandyKnowe, just across the river. Thomas Dodds and Walter had played together when they were children, but Walter was a sickly child, rarely coming outside when he was young. Consequently, he was schooled at the manor house, and Thomas would come and visit him. Now Walter was a man, and the writings he did while a captive in the house were beginning to sell.

Loving this land, Walter had built Abbotsford House across the river from the Doddses and hired Jenny as his housekeeper. Walter Scott took pride in knowing everyone in the neighborhood, including the children. On his horse, Covenanter, with his great deer hound, Maida, he rode up to all the cottages and spoke to everyone as though they were blood relations. His friend, Shortreed, sometimes rode with him, and folks could hear their laughter and banter far ahead of their cottages No longer ill, Walter Scott made up for being confined by becoming an avid hunter, rider, and outdoorsman.

The next morning, Walter and Shortreed rode up to Thomas Dodds, who was fixing a broken plow. "Morning, Thomas," Walter shouted as they approached.

"Morning, Walter. What brings you over today?"

"Oh, nothing; just visiting."

"Well come on in then. Helen just finished her shortbread biscuits."

Walter and Shortreed looked at each other. "Oh, yes, don't have to ask us twice." With that, they entered the little cottage.

The children were eating their porridge, and Ann was staring strangely at her sister, Jenny. Somehow, Ann knew everything that went on around the countryside, so she suspected Jenny had a beau who was none other than Walter Scott's nephew, John Scott, son to Lord Henry Scott who owned half the countryside. She had never seen them together but knew her sister had been secretive and giddy the last few times she had come home from working at Walter Scott's manor. Those times had been when John was home. Of course, any union of marriage was forbidden between the two. Though Thomas Dodds was a master carpenter and journeyman and worked for patrons as far north as Galashiels and as far south as Jedburgh, about eight miles in either direction, the family was not royalty or gentry. Marriage was forbidden between working class and gentry.

Jenny and John had met months earlier just before the silo incident when she hired on to clean Walter Scott's manor. John came to spend late spring and summer with his Uncle Walter. Upon entering the library, through the open door, he saw the back of a young woman who was kneeling with her head in the large stone fireplace. "Good Morning, Lass."

Jenny jerked out of the fireplace and struck her head on the top of the opening. "Ow," she cried, turning to see who was there and holding her head at the same time. Standing before her was a boy with the most beautiful hair she had ever seen. It flowed in soft yellow waves down to his shoulders and shined like gold in the morning sun.

"Oh, I'm so sorry, Lass. I didn't mean to startle you." He rushed toward her, grabbing her arm and helping her the rest of the way up.

"Uh, yes, yes, I am fine; I am fine, I think," Jenny replied as she brushed the soot off her once white apron. "Uh, what do you…. Who are you?" she stammered.

"Oh, forgive me. I am John Scott. I am visiting my uncle for the summer. I didn't mean to startle you."

Jenny stood transfixed. She could not take her eyes off him. His eyes were sky blue and stood above a prominent straight Scottish nose. The boy wore a red plaid tartan flat cap, green knickers, and a green vest. Jenny became painfully aware that her face was smudged and her hair was stuck in strands to her face. Quickly, she began pushing the pieces of hair into her cap "I am Jenny Dodds. I clean for your uncle."

"I see that," John replied, too stunned by her natural beauty to speak more than a three-word sentence. Jet-black strands of hair stuck

28

to the palest skin he had ever seen. Soot blackened her turned-up nose, and he could not help but smile as she tried frantically to wipe her face clean, only smudging it more. "I came in here because I cannot find the cook, and I am hungry."

Jenny wondered if his uncle knew he was coming. Surely, he would have arranged for a cook to be there. The cooks were always in attendance when Mr. Scott was there. "John, the cook is not coming until this afternoon. Didn't your uncle know you were coming?"

"Yes, he did, but sometimes he gets lost in his writing and forgets details such as eating and that his nephew is arriving." He laughed as he handed his backpack and coat to Charles, the butler, who had arrived upon hearing young John.

Jenny loved John's Uncle Walter's writings especially the romantic ones like "Lockinvar," about a knight who comes back from war only to arrive on the day of his love's marriage.

"Well, I know the cook, and I don't think she would mind if I fixed you something." John followed her into the kitchen. She found eggs, leftover haggis, and a slab of pork, which she sliced for bacon. She sent John into the dining hall and soon came out with a plateful of delicious smelling food. She set the plate down and turned to go back to cleaning.

"Can you sit with me while I eat?"

"Well, I really need to finish up here as I have chores waiting at home."

"How about I finish up here and you sit with me?"

"You?" She couldn't imagine a grandson of Charles Montagu Scott, Duke of Buccleuch, cleaning a fireplace or doing any manual labor. "But...."

"I know you think I can't do it, but I have not lived a privileged life. My father and my uncle do not get along, and most of the estate was left to my Uncle Walter. My father was in love with the pubs and the gin in them, which quickly ate away all our money. Though Uncle Walter refused to lend him more money, he did offer to take me, which enraged my father to the point of forbidding me to see him. In the meantime, my mum and I had to work to eat. Mum took in washing, and I worked as an apprentice for a blacksmith. Well that is a piece of my sad story, the point being that I too have been black from head to foot, and I too can clean a fireplace. Now, will you sit with me?"

She did, and as late spring folded into summer, John would come to know when she walked the narrow thistle-lined path to the little stone schoolhouse where she taught. He would meet her in the wooded glen beneath the crooked beech trees that lined the creek.

Jenny began to live for those moments. A touch of his arm on hers sent chills through her body. She had never felt anything like this before. She lay awake at night dreaming of the special moment when they would kiss. It would be her first kiss. Some days she could not wait and guiltily sent the children home early. Then she would make an excuse to run to Abbotsford to see him. They found a special place in the glen, an abandoned cottage. She knew it was a notable risk because her father would forbid her to see John if he found out. If Lord

Scott knew, he could kick her family out of the tenant cottage, and now since the lowland clearances, there were fewer and fewer jobs for tenant farmers. Though modern ideas were coming to Scotland, gentry and the commoner were still forbidden to marry. She knew they would have to stop seeing each other, but every afternoon there she was, waiting for him, her heart pounding at the sound of his footsteps on the stone path. When he wrapped his arms around her, she would think, "Well, no one knows, and he will be gone at the end of summer," and when he kissed her, there was no thought, no class difference, and no rules. All that existed in that kiss was the way it made her feel in the moment with his open hand on her back and the other caressing her face. She never wanted it to stop.

One afternoon as the two lovers sat on the bank of the River Tweed watching the waters curl and play in the summer breeze, they did not know that an intruder was watching. Running along the giant stone wall in front of Wright Bryden's farm about 50 feet from the Tweed bank, Ann Dodds looked over at the craggy alders reaching their crooked fingers into the sky. When she was a child, those trees had frightened her. She thought they were witches turned to wood by a magic spell. Suddenly, a movement among the branches caught her eye. She saw a flash of red and at first thought it was a rooster broken away from its pen, but when she squinted her eyes, she realized it was a red cap. Jumping down from the wall, she crouched down and began to move closer. Soon she could make out a young man and woman stopped on the path. Curious, she creeped through the yarrow then hid behind a swaying birch tree. She soon recognized her sister and the

Scott boy who stayed with his uncle. After watching for what seemed like ten minutes, nothing happened—no holding hands no kissing or touching. 'They are just two friends,' she thought, 'who met on the path and stopped to talk.'

Ann had met John Scott and judged him a kind person, though she didn't really like any boys. Her auburn pigtails flew up as she raced through the field to catch up to them. Then, before her very eyes, John slowly reached out and took Jenny's hand. Ann stopped and stared. She couldn't believe what she was seeing; now they were holding hands, facing each other, and looking deep into each other's eyes the way Da and Ma sometimes looked at each other. Ann took a deep breath and covered her mouth with her hand. She was too close. She did not want them to hear her, but they did. Immediately, they pulled their hands away and Jenny yelled, "What are you doing here?"

"Just playing," Ann replied, coming alongside them.

"You mean spying. You were spying on me!"

"I wasn't, swear I wasn't, but I saw you; I saw you holding hands; holding hands with a Scott!"

"And you will tell no one. You hear me? You will tell no one!" cried Jenny.

"I never said I would, did I?"

"No, but Ann you can't; you just can't, or John and I will both be in trouble."

"Are, are you, ah, together?"

"No, Ann, we are not together. We are friends."

"Friends don't hold hands."

"Some do," Jenny replied. "I've seen you hold hands with your friend, Sarah."

"Yes, a girl, and I was six years old." Ann was not a dull wit. "Don't try to trick me, and don't lie. If you do, I will tell." With that, John and Jenny sat down with Ann and told her that they had been meeting for some time, and when she reminded them that they could never marry, they told her that they knew that; they were just seeing each other through the summer. John would be leaving in the fall to attend university, and then it would end.

Ann looked at them and then glanced over at the Tweed, watching it saunter over the white rocks bouncing on the bottom: water so clear and pure, never halting for a branch or boulder. Uh huh, it would end at the finish of summer, they said. 'It will end,' Ann thought, 'but not because of summer,' and that is how she became a messenger in this love affair.

Gail Huntley

CHAPTER IV
1817

In the howling headwinds of winter, news of the Rutherfords' fall reached the Doddses' household. As the Industrial Revolution made its way across the borders of Scotland, it left in its wake lost jobs, starvation, and immigration to the land called America. Though the barons of the castles kept much of their wealth, the cost of keeping tenants to run the farms began to outweigh the need. A machine could do the work of three men, making it cost effective for the lairds of the manors to let their tenants go. In some cases, even the lairds fell on tough times as the cost of running the enormous estates surpassed family wealth and income from the lands. Sadly, the Rutherfords found themselves in this situation in February of the year 1817. It was a bleak time in the borders of Scotland as the snow piled up against the stone pillars of the Rutherford estate. No longer able to make a living, starvation loomed like a black cloud over the large family of seven children. On a chilly February day, Jenny Dodds came upon one of the Rutherford children peeking through the window of the Doddses' cottage. She stopped, realizing it was six-year-old Fiona Rutherford. "My, my, little one, so what are you doing so far from home on this wintry day?" She squatted down to make herself eye level with this child whose blond curls were poking out from the rim of her sheepskin hat.

"I'm hungry," the little girl cried.

"Well, well, we mustn't let those tears freeze out here. Come inside with me, Fiona."

"Oh, no, no. Da would be angry if he knew I was here."

"I don't think your da would be angry if I invited you in; besides, I am cold and need to go in. Come on." Fiona reluctantly entered the Doddses' house where the full story came out: how the Rutherfords had to leave because there was no more bread or potatoes. Little Fiona gobbled up the big plate of food Helen prepared for her. Jenny was astonished at how rapidly she consumed the food.

When she finished, Helen gathered together a sack full of potatoes and a ring of haggis she had just made. "We will see you home, Fiona," Jenny told her.

"No, you cannot. You cannot," cried Fiona, "me mum will be mad."

"She will be mad at us, Fiona, not you. Now, let's get your coat on and start out," Helen coaxed. Ann and Robert hooked up the horse to the one-seated sleigh, and Helen, Jenny, and Fiona began the twenty-minute trek to the Rutherfords' through the snow-ladened field. Helen and Jenny were amazed that Fiona had walked through snow that was up to her knees to get to their house. Jenny carried her to the steps of the Rutherford home. Helen knocked on the door and waited. She knocked again, and after a few minutes Rachel Rutherford opened the door. Her blond hair was flying out from a quickly made bun, and her eyes at once found Fiona. "Oh, my goodness, Fiona; where have you been? We have been searching everywhere for you child!" She reached out and pulled Fiona in. "Oh my, Helen, thank you, but where did you find her?" She held Fiona to her, and after Helen explained where they had found her, Rachel thanked them for bringing her home. She did not invite them in.

After an awkward few minutes, Helen asked if they could come in and warm up before returning home. Rachel's behavior was not typical of Scottish hospitality. Receiving visitors was an honor, and they would always be invited in. Thinking about what Fiona had told them, Helen pushed on. "Rachel, we are very cold, and I must rest before going back."

"Oh, of course," Rachel said, opening the door wider, so Jenny and Helen could enter. What they saw, or did not see, shocked them; there was nothing in the hall or great room. There was no furniture, not even wall hangings or curtains.

"Rachel, what…?" Helen asked, looking at Rachel and then into the room.

Rachel began unbuttoning Fiona's jacket. When she finished, after hugging her one more time, she sent her upstairs to her room. Three other children, all under the age of six, crowded around Rachel, hiding behind her skirts. Silas, the twelve-year-old, stood against the wall. "Silas, take the children upstairs." As soon as they were in their bedrooms, Rachel's tears began. She told them how the bill collectors had come and taken everything. She explained that Richard's brother, Theodore—who had inherited the estate when their father, Ben

Rutherford, died—had gambled away much of the money. Richard had not known the seriousness of Theodore's problem until one night some horrible men began beating on their door. Richard opened it, and the men told him they were looking for his brother and why. Either Richard would tell them where he was, or they would harm me and the children. Richard persuaded them to take the money instead. They had agreed to take the money, but it left the Rutherfords with barely enough to live on, so with the little they had left, Richard had bought fare to America. They would sail in six weeks. In the meantime, they had used up most of their food, and because of the deep snow they could not gather enough wood for adequate heat. "I fear for our very lives, and I am so ashamed that Fiona came to your house searching for food."

Helen was in shock. She could not believe what had happened to this family. "Where is Theodore now? Can't he pay you back?"

"We have not heard a word, and he has moved from his last place. We don't know if he is dead or is hiding from us and those bad men. Again, I am so sorry Fiona did this…."

"No, no, I am glad she did," Helen said. "Please, we are longtime friends, and I wish we had known sooner. I must tell Thomas. He will want to help."

"No, no, Richard would kill me if he knew I told you."

"And your Rutherford pride will kill all of you if you don't do something, Rachel." Jenny brought in the food from their home; Rachel thanked them, and Helen convinced her to let Thomas talk with Richard about helping them. That night Thomas made the trip to the

Rutherfords' and spoke with Richard. After much talking and reminding this proud man of his children's and wife's needs, they devised a plan: the Rutherfords would move in with the Doddses until their ship left in six weeks.

The small Rutherford children bunked in the loft with the Doddses' brood while the older children, along with Richard and Rachel Rutherford, slept in the barn. The Rutherfords were a proud highland clan and could not believe their misfortune. In the night, as they lay atop the hay, Rachel Rutherford whispered to her husband, "Richard, what is to become of us? To think that it was not that long ago that we owned one of the most beautiful estates in the valley."

"Yes, Rachel, I am so sorry to have brought this upon you and the children."

"Oh, but 'tis not your fault, dear, please don't ever think that I blame you. It is the times and besides, we are going to America. Beatrice says they are doing well and have a fine piece of land in a place called New York." Beatrice was Rachel's sister, and her family had made the trip the year before. The journey over on the ship had been very difficult and when they set foot on soil in Newfoundland, Beatrice said they thanked God.

"Yes, we will go to America, and we will be okay," Richard assured his wife. However, he did not reveal that the ticket would take most of the money they had saved so they would not be able to buy anything on the way or once they got there. Thank goodness Beatrice and William were letting them stay with them in the new land.

Richard Rutherford and Thomas had lived side by side for years. Though Richard had attended a different school, they had played together as children. Now, it was understood that their relationship would end on the day of their departure. And so it was that the next month they held a funeral service at the Lessudden Church for the Rutherfords. The whole town attended the funeral to say goodbye to the family. Funerals were held because it was known that the families going overseas would never return.

The Rutherfords left on a bright spring morning in 1817. The Doddses took them to the station where they would board the horse-drawn carriage that would take them to Greenock where they would board ship. Helen gave them as much food as they could spare. Helen hugged little Fiona and placed a bag in her tiny hand. "These are for you, wee one." Fiona looked inside and saw her favorite biscuits.

"Thank you, Mrs. Dodds."

"You are welcome, Fiona. Have fun on the big ship."

"It's scary."

"Oh, I think ships are beautiful, and it will take you to a beautiful new land." Fiona turned and took her mother's hand and entered the carriage. Helen said a prayer for the Rutherford clan.

Months went by and they heard nothing from the family. Helen inquired at the maritime office many times, and, mysteriously, they had no records of their ship landing on the shores of Northumberland. Helen wrote to her Aunt Catherine and Uncle Wright in America, but they had not seen the Rutherfords. "We will think well and know that they are in America somewhere. It is a big country," Thomas remarked.

"Yes, but I don't understand why there is no letter," Helen replied. Every day she checked the mail, but no letter arrived. However, what did arrive was a notice from the Laird of Buccleuch informing Thomas that starting in June, his rent would be raised. Thomas knew there was little money left at the end of the month to pay rent, and now he feared that they would become paupers. If the farm work ended, he knew they could not live on the money from his carpentry business. In addition, Helen's weaving and spinning no longer brought in much extra money because she could not compete with the machine-made clothes flooding the shops. The machines produced clothes so fast that merchants had to drop suppliers like Helen to compete with other merchants. The children were already contributing what they could. Consequently, it was decided that Wright Bryden would hire eleven-year-old Robert to work on the manor.

Thomas called his son into the barn to meet with Wright, "Robert, you know Baron Bryden?"

"Yes, Da."

"Starting tomorrow you will go to the Baron's place and work. You will do whatever he asks of you. Do you understand?"

"I am to work like Ann and Jenny?"

"Yes, Robert."

"And get a wage?"

"Robert! That is not to be asked now!"

"No, Thomas, 'tis fine. It shows the lad is thinking. Yes, Robert, I will pay you two pounds per week."

"Thank you, Wright, that will be fine, and I understand he will work after school and on Saturday."

"So, he will be there from 1:00 PM to 7:00 PM during the week and 8:00 AM to 7:00 PM on Saturday with Sunday off for the Sabbath. So, Robert, will I see you tomorrow?"

"Yes, Baron, I can do that," Robert beamed. Finally, he was old enough to do what Ann and Jenny did. Tom had to stay at home and work with his father, so now the three oldest would be working. Thomas felt terrible about the long hours, but he dared not say anything as Wright was known for his temper. They needed the money, so he could not afford to lose favor with Wright Bryden. Helen was furious.

"How is he to get his school work done? He must have more time to eat his dinner and do his studies," Helen lamented to Thomas.

"Helen, we need the money," Thomas pleaded. "I don't want to do this, but if not, we will not survive next winter." Helen looked at her little boy. His blue eyes shown with pride as he told her he was going to help the family. She vowed to do something, anything, to change this horrible situation. She knew that soon Robert would realize what he had to give up—playing ball with his friends, fishing, running through the glen, swimming in the loch, and hunting.

The next day, Helen headed out across the field soon after Thomas drove off in the buckboard to Jedburgh. She tied the baby to her chest and began the two-mile trek to the Bryden farm. As she

42

approached the large stone house, her breathing quickened. Fear crept through her as she lifted the knocker on the large wooden door surrounded by stone blocks that reached far into the sky. She had met Sara Bryden a few times at the local market, at the fair, and on one occasion when the baroness had purchased one of Helen's handmade baskets. Baroness Sara Bryden was well off by normal standards. She was a Stewart coming from the Gordon clan who owned most of the eastern highlands. The Brydens had no children, though they had tried for years to have a child. This was a problem, since all holdings were passed on to the sons or daughters to run the manor. A gray-haired woman with a starched white hat and apron opened the door. "Hello, may I help you?"

"Yes, I am Helen and would like to speak to Baroness Bryden."

"Is she expecting you?"

"No."

"Very well; I will tell her." She left leaving Helen standing outside the door. A few minutes later, the door opened, and the maid said, "Baroness Bryden will see you. Please follow me." She led Helen to a grand hall with floor-to-ceiling windows surrounded by heavy burgundy drapes. The maid motioned Helen to sit down then quietly disappeared. Helen sat down on a mahogany chair. She knew that it was one of Thomas' chairs Wright had commissioned him to make. After waiting for what seemed like an hour, the baroness appeared dressed in a white shirt, beige riding pants, and boots. Helen was shocked. Who was this woman in men's clothes? Surely not the mistress of the house.

"Good Morning, Mrs. Dodds." Sara had met the Doddses children and had seen the family at the local fair. She knew Thomas, since he and Baron Bryden helped each other out at times with issues on their farms, and though she knew Helen from purchasing baskets and biscuits from her at the fair, she was startled to find her at her door.

"Good morning, Baroness."

"Sara, please, Sara, but, my goodness, did I order something from you?"

"No, Baroness, uh Sara, you did not. I am here on another matter."

"Do come in, dear." She ushered Helen into a lavish sitting room and instructed the maid to bring them tea.

"Oh no, please, I do not wish to impose. I will not be long."

"Hush, hush, it is not often I have a visitor. Please stay and state your reason for coming." Helen, though terrified, began to relax a little and plundered on about her young son coming to work there and how the hours were so long that he would not be able to do his studies. Sara listened and replied, "I understand, but your husband does require him to work, correct?"

"Oh, yes, and he did not dare speak up to your husband about the matter for fear he would change his mind and not hire my boy at all."

"Well, yes, yes, Wright can be a bit impetuous, and I do understand your concern, Mrs. Dodds, but I don't know if I can do anything about it."

"I just thought maybe you could talk with your husband and see if Robert could start at 3:00 PM instead of 1:00 PM so he can eat his dinner and do his studies." Sara did understand, but Wright was a stubborn man; however, she did agree to talk to her husband about the matter. Two days later, Robert came in for his evening dinner and told Helen that Wright Bryden had changed his hours. Helen smiled; if either husband knew that Helen had interfered, he would be angry. Sara and Helen would carry that secret for the rest of their lives.

Gail Huntley

CHAPTER V

1817

It was another year before the Doddses and the Rules began feeling the pinch of tough times in Scotland. Other Scottish families who had migrated to America were writing home about freedom. Still others were buying up land and selling it as fertile farmland in this promised land of abundance.

The population of Great Britain had doubled in the last century. Disappearing jobs along with an increasing population caused the government to begin looking at the new land as an opportunity to solve the problem; hence, the government began urging tenant farmers to move to the colonies. To entice them, some government-sponsored companies offered free parcels of land or free passage with a pledge to work for those landowners in the colonies. Throughout Great Britain, people such as William Corbett and Washington Irving were calling for the cleaning up of rotten boroughs, parliamentary reform, and an end to suffrage. Only the gentry voted, but now the rest of the people wanted to vote, and just across the ocean was a ready-made republic.

On the other hand, promoters of upper Canada protested the decision (by those who were deluded, as the Canadians viewed it, by the lure of democracy and fertile land) to forsake their British allegiance and pass through Canada into the United States. They warned immigrants that in America you had to own a slave or be one. These stories and confusion added to the stress of choosing a life of known poverty or unknown risk. These were the thoughts of Thomas Dodds when he and his sons were hunting in the Scotland hills. In the pubs, Thomas heard stories about the voyages from Scotland to Canada and then Canada to America. Newspapers were full of accounts of shipwrecks, illnesses, and starvation when rough seas caused delays and passengers ran out of food. The ships sailed from Scotland to Newfoundland. Some people settled there, others moved further into Canada settling in Montreal or Quebec, others sailed down the St. Lawrence to places along that mighty river; some were never heard from again.

In America, the American Revolution ended in 1783, but it did not end in northern New York until 1797, when the Jay Treaty was ratified. Until then, the St. Lawrence valley was not safe for settlers. Because the population was getting too large in England, the British government encouraged people to go to the colonies anyway. They emptied the debtors' prisons and shipped the inmates off to this new uncivilized land they named the 'promised land.' Going there was not always a positive endeavor, but that news did not reach the peasants or prisoners or dreamers. The Doddses and Rules did not know that there were still British garrisons all along the St. Lawrence River and that British officers were encouraging the Indians to frighten pioneers away, forcing some of them to move on or move back, with many dying on the return trip. They also did not know that panthers, bear, and bobcats roamed the wilds of northern New York where many of them were headed. However, though mail from America was intermittent at best, a few letters did reach the Doddses and their neighbors. Wright Rule wrote Thomas describing their trip across the Atlantic to Newfoundland, into Canada, then down the St. Lawrence River, and into the land called New York.

One afternoon, when Thomas returned from hunting, Helen handed him a letter she had received from her Aunt Catherine Rule. The letter described living in America. She wrote about how men like Alexander Macomb, Robert Morris, David Parish, and the Hollande Land Company were selling enormous land purchases in New York State. Wright had purchased several acres from Mr. Parish on loan and was now working his own farm. Thomas stood in his barn and read how every man voted, regardless of whether he owned land, and how land could be owned by any man regardless of class. The next day when Thomas went into the local store, he asked Frederick the owner what he had heard about America.

"Oh, yes, they're all talking about it now. We got these pamphlets from there the other day." Frederick pointed to the thin pamphlet on the counter.

Another patron chimed in, "Yup, says there is lots of cheap farmland if you're just willing to make the trip to some place up in that New York State." Thomas picked up the ad and scanned it.

"Yes, but isn't there still fighting up there with the French and Indians?"

"Don't know," replied another old timer, pipe in his mouth, "but I heard they have cats the size of horses in those towering mountains up there on the Canadian border."

"Can't believe everything you hear, though," Thomas shot back.

"No, you can't, but I'm not going. Heard some of the young Scott boy's family is going to purchase some land there, though."

"You mean John, the boy that stays with Walter in the summer?"

"Yes, that family."

"Hmm, heard he is off to college next year."

"That's right," Franklin added; "he is going to Oxford, they say, and staying on holidays with his uncle."

"Ah, such is the luxury of the well to do. Not the Doddses' lot, though. Well, got to get home." Thomas picked up his salt and cloth for Helen and left. As he rode through the alder trees and looked out over the valley, he thought, 'this is my home, but this is not my valley. How would it be to say, this is my valley?' A decision was forming, but he needed to speak with his father.

He turned the cart around and headed back to town, pulled up in front of the jail and walked in. His father looked up at him from the desk. "Well hello, Thomas. Good to see you."

"You too, Da. You got any bad guys back there?" He peered into the two cells.

"Nope, just released old Charlie Tucker, though." Charlie always drank too much and sometimes got wild and ended up in jail sleeping it off.

"I need to talk to you about something."

"Okay, son, what is it?"

"Well, uh, I, ah…."

"Spit it out, Thomas. Just spit it out. What's on your mind?"

"Have you heard news from the colonies?"

"Oh, thought maybe that was it."

"What? What do you mean?"

"Well, I know what's going on. Them machines taking over our jobs. Talk in the pub is that even the lairds are in trouble, so I knew you might be."

"We are. We just can't make ends meet, Da, and we have received letters about how you can own your own land in America."

"Yup, I heard that too, but don't know as I'd believe it all, and what about the trip over? It is not an easy one, you know, and do you have money saved up to buy this land?"

"No, but I heard you can work for a company or an owner for a few years and then they release the land to you, and I heard they will give you a loan."

"You heard. You heard. Do you know?"

"Well only from Helen's uncle, one of the Rules."

"Uh huh, the one that was arrested for horse thievery and escaped to this new land?"

Thomas smiled. Bringing up this uncle somehow made people do that. Reality was that this man was accused of being a criminal, but he was so generous and so happy most of the time that people tended to overlook his crime. Thomas looked down at the floor and shuffled his feet. "I know, but it isn't just him. There are others."

51

"Who?"

"Just others."

"Like the Rutherfords who left, and disappeared probably into the ocean?"

"No, Father, we finally received word. They were lost in Canada and ended up in a place called Crown Point on a Lake Champlain in New York. There was no place they could post a letter. I forgot to tell you and look, Da, I have a map." Thomas and his father poured over the map picking out the route the family would take to Newfoundland and onto the St. Lawrence River. When Thomas left, his father was still against his idea but gave him his blessing. He watched his son walk out the door knowing he had made up his mind. Fear rippled through him as he resigned himself to the reality that this family he had created would soon be gone forever. He and Ellen would never see them again once they left Scotland.

It took Thomas more time and thought before he was sure enough to talk with Helen about his plan. He swore his father to secrecy while he made up his mind.

"You bought what?" Helen gasped as she learned that Thomas had spent money on a map of the new world of all things. "You think spending money on a map is more important than buying boots for George who needs them right now?"

"Yes, I do. Sit down, Helen, and listen."

That was the night they decided. Helen offered all the sensible arguments against going, such as the danger, the children's schooling, no money once they got there, and leaving behind everything they had ever known. She was terrified. "Thomas, I don't think I can do this." She knew, according to the church, that she was to follow her husband where he went, but this was different; this was too much to ask. And that was another thing, were there even churches in this place?

Thomas had answers for most of her fears, assuring her that many people had now crossed the ocean and were doing well in the new land. "Read this pamphlet, Helen; we could have our own land. Oh, to get up in the morning and know that the land I till would be my own; can you just imagine?" Helen looked at the way her husband's face lit up as he stared out the open door looking at a dream. This man who worked so hard mending fences, traveling miles to build a house, repairing wheels, chopping wood at the light of dawn, and coming in late at night falling asleep before dinner in his chair. She too stared out the window. What did he have for all his toil? He had someone else's house to come to after working all day. She could not deny her husband this chance—or her children, as this would also be their future. Helen walked over to her husband and cupped his tear-stained face with her palms. She looked into his tired brown eyes and said, "We will go, love; we will go."

"Really, Helen, really? You want to go too?"

"I do not, dear, but we are losing what we have here. The future is bleak. I have fears—the voyage across the sea, leaving all we have ever known, the foreboding wildness of this new land, but if this Aunt Catherine's letter is true and what the other letters I hear about are true, then we must go."

"Ah, my Helen," Thomas cooed as he picked her up and swung her around. They both laughed. "We are going! We are going!"

"Where are we going?" Jenny asked, as she stood frozen in the doorway. "Da, just where are we going?"

CHAPTER VI

Jenny could not believe what she was hearing. After her father repeated his plan, she was speechless. She turned and ran out the door, tears streaming down her cheeks. She flew through the dry winter heather not feeling it scratching at her ankles. She ran straight to John, who was home on holiday, frantically banging on his door. "John, John, open the door!" She heard the latch click and there he was standing before her.

"What, what is it, Jenny? Are you hurt? Did something happen?" By this time, Charles and Walter had joined John at the door.

"Yes, something is wrong, very wrong. We are moving."

"What? Moving! Where? In town?"

"No, I wish. To America. We are moving to America!" Jenny lamented, barely hearing what she was saying.

"What?" John asked, thinking he had not heard right. He stood there dumbstruck staring at Jenny.

Uncle Walter interrupted, "Come in. Come in, Lass." He turned to Charles, "Please get this girl a glass of water and bring us some tea, Charles."

"Yes Sir." Charles replied, quickly tending to the task.

The three sat down, and Jenny told them how her parents had made the decision to leave in the spring. Trying to lighten the girl's sadness, Walter reiterated how he had been to the colonies and loved the beauty and vastness of the land. "Jenny, Lass, the people there are happier, and there are large rivers and lakes like here." Jenny did not want to hear any of it. She could care less about all that. "I don't care about that. It doesn't matter; I'm not going anyway."

"I will leave you two to talk on your own," Walter said as he stood up. "John, see to it that Jenny gets home safely."

"I will, uncle."

"John, I am not going. I am not going. This is my home. This is my land. How can they just up and leave?"

"What do you mean, love? You have to go with your family."

"But, John, what will happen to us?"

"I don't know, Lass, but you are not old enough to stay on your own."

"Yes, I am. I can teach school and live here."

"But you would need a better job to get a flat in town, and everybody wants jobs right now. They go to the men with families. Oh, my Lord, but I would miss you terribly. I thought it was bad enough leaving you during the school year, but this is much worse."

"I know. We must do something."

"Maybe you can talk them out of it."

"Or, maybe I could stay with Grandpa and grandma Rule in Jedburgh. Yes, that is it." Jenny's mind raced, "I would not be able to run over here, but it is only an hour away on horseback. I could get a job or help them in the store. I am past eighteen and should be married anyway, except…."

"I know, except for me. Oh, Jenny, I want to marry you, but you know I can't."

Jenny was running out of answers. Filled with fear, she blurted out, "Why can't we? You say your parents would disown you; they want you to marry the Gordon woman they have chosen for you, but what if you don't? What if you marry me instead?"

"My Lass, I want to marry you, but we are so young. I can't. My parents would take everything away including Oxford, not to mention my responsibilities being the oldest son. I am expected to inherit and run the manor when my parents pass. Oh, Jen, I want to be with you more than you know, but…."

"I know. I know, John. I have known since the first time we met. I'm sorry. How rude of me to pressure you. I know I have to let you go, but it is so hard," she cried as he held her. "John, without you, I will have no life. I will never marry if that is what it takes to keep seeing you." She reached up and put her arms around his neck, and they kissed, melting into each other with the passion of lovers torn apart and rejoined in their mind's eye.

John took Jenny home on Covenanter. She clung to him as ivy clings to a great oak, breathing in the scent she had come to love. In the patch of alders at the edge of the field, he got off the horse, helped Jenny off, embraced her, and kissed her long and hard. Once again, Jenny felt the heat rising in her body as she became limp in his arms.

She pulled away and lost herself in his sea-blue eyes. "John Scott, I love you," she declared.

"Jenny Dodds, I love you, too." They embraced and kissed one last time before continuing home. As she watched John disappear over the hill, Jenny began conjuring up a way to convince her parents to let her stay in Jedburgh.

Upon entering the cottage, all the children came up to her. "Did you hear," Ann asked, "that we are going to America?"

"Yes, I heard, and I think it is stupid."

"Why?"

"Because we belong here. Scotland is our home."

"But Da says it will be better there. We can have our own land," Robert chimed in excitedly.

"And Da can do what they call vote in the new country," Ann offered.

"I don't care, and I don't want to hear it!" Jenny shouted covering her ears and running out the door slamming it in her sister's face. She wanted to be alone. Why were they happy about leaving? Well, they could all move. She was moving to Jedburgh!

"Janet Dodds, you get back in here and close that door quietly," chided her mother. "I understand you don't want to leave. I don't either, but times are tough here, and we need to make a living if we all want to continue eating; so, young lady, instead of being angry and feeling sorry for yourself, you might come in here and help with supper."

"Yes, ma'am," Jenny whispered, stomping back through the door but closing it quietly. She would tell them her plans tomorrow. They would not go anyway. They had the whole winter to change their minds. Maybe the laird would not let her da go in the spring. Maybe her ma would sell more linens. Besides, if they were so poor where would Da get the money for passage?

Jenny did not know that Da already had most of the money for passage because he had agreed to work in America for a man named Parish who owned land in New York. Mr. Parish would pay for his passage if Thomas worked for him for two years. She did not know then that in just a few short months she would look long and hard at her sisters and brothers and be torn apart by a decision she would make.

Gail Huntley

CHAPTER VII
1818–1819

Dawn broke badly on that September morning in 1818 when John left for Oxford. Rain beat down on Jenny as she stood in the alders watching him ride away from her. Only an hour earlier, they had lain on a blanket in the heather at the foot of Eildon Hills and kissed for the last time until Christmas break.

"We will write, my love," John whispered as he kissed her tear-stained cheek.

Jenny could not hide her disappointment, even though she knew it was her own fault for getting involved with John in the first place. She looked up at him, "Why, John? Why would we write? There is no future for us, so maybe we should say goodbye right now for good."

"If that is what you want, Lass, I will not write."

"No, John, please, yes, please write." To have no word from each other was too painful, so as he boarded the carriage and hugged her, he said, whispering in her ear, "I will send letters to Lucille for you. She knows." Lucille Walton was Jenny's best friend.

"I will read every letter over and over," she cried. She held up the paper he had given her with his address written on it and vowed to write him every day He boarded the carriage, and she watched until all that was left was the dust spewing up from the wagon wheels. Then, her life became one of waiting, for letters, for Christmas break when he would return to SandyKnowe, for hope that loomed above her like a silver sword. Later, she would learn to hate hope and all the disappointments it carried on its back.

In the meantime, her mother encouraged her to meet the young men in town. It was past time for Jenny to be married. One night, just before dinner, there was a knock on the door. "Jenny, would you get that, please," Helen called. Jenny climbed down the loft stairs and opened the door. There stood Fergus Walton, the local blacksmith.

"Hello, Jenny, you look pretty tonight."

"Ah, Fergus, thank you. What, what can we do for you?"

"You didn't know? Your ma invited me to dinner."

"Oh, no, no, I didn't. Come in. come in." She glared at her mother as she announced that Fergus had arrived. She knew her mother was up to matchmaking, and she wanted no part of it. She shoved John's latest letter deep into her apron pocket and led the man to a chair at the table. Jenny had known him all her life. Lucille, her best friend, and Fergus were cousins, and they all went to the same church. She was a little nervous that Lucille's parents could find out about her and John from Lucille, but Lucille had agreed to keep the secret, and Jenny trusted her. Fergus' family lived outside Lessudden. His father, Thomas Walton, was a maltster who produced malt for brewers and at one time owned twelve houses in Leeds. His wife, Mary, came from a large wealthy family who lived in a two-story ten-room stone dwelling surrounded by a garden of lush red rhododendrons.

Though Mary Walton had wealth before she married Thomas, she put her money in trust to an accountant named Peter Thompson who promptly spent all of it. In 1795, when Thomas Walton's first daughter was born Thomas and Mary became embroiled in a legal battle with Thompson, who now had no money to pay them back. So, though the Walton family was much wealthier than the Doddses and classed as gentry, the fact that Helen Rule Dodds' great grandfather, John, married a royal Stuart put their families on somewhat equal grounding. Hence, Fergus was an eligible mate for Jenny.

Jenny sat opposite her guest and politely said to Fergus, "I am so glad you could come."

"Thank you, Mrs. Dodds, for inviting me."

When the meal was ready, Helen instructed Fergus to sit next to Jenny. They ate dinner, and when they finished, Helen suggested they all retire to the front porch. Soon Helen put the children to bed and beckoned Thomas to come inside, leaving Jenny and Fergus sitting alone on the porch swing. Fergus talked about school and family, and Jenny listened. It was not that she did not like Fergus or that he wasn't interesting to talk with; she felt uncomfortable being alone with another man.

She began to tell Fergus about her parents' plan to move to America. He listened intently and said he understood and that he would not want to leave his homeland no matter what. Sitting looking out over the meadow, listening to the hoot owls in the distance on this silent crisp November night, Jenny began to tell him about John Scott. She had no idea why, but suddenly the words tumbled out like an avalanche, words that had been bottled up for so long, and when she finished, and the tears dried, instead of fleeing, Fergus Walton bent down and gently kissed her, and she did not back away. She was in shock that she had just told him a secret that could destroy anything she had left with John.

Fergus put his arm around her, pulled the blanket up over them, and said, "Jenny, I am so sorry you are hurt. I only wish I could take your pain away. I have liked you since we were in first grade, but I was too shy to tell you. You are so beautiful, and I knew you would never consent to courting me, so I have courted you in my dreams. Now, I know your heart is with another, and I respect that, but could I see you again, maybe for a walk?"

Jenny agreed to walk with Fergus after church the next Sunday and several Sundays after that. It was a relief to talk to someone about her feelings. She was amazed that he never tried to stop her, though she spoke less and less about John as she witnessed the pain it brought to Fergus' large brown eyes. There were suppers at the Doddses' and suppers at the Walton house, and soon Jenny was looking forward to seeing him come over the rise. They always had things to talk about—customers coming into his blacksmith shop, school years, the Lessudden fair, and America. Fergus found books in the library about America and brought them to Jenny. She read them out loud, and they learned about the colonies, how each one had a governor, and how the first people settled in Virginia. They learned about Jamestown, the

64

American Revolution, and the defeat of the British. They discussed how the Americans would feel about emigrants coming from Scotland, Ireland, and England. Would they be hostile? Were the Indians still hostile? They sat in church and at socials together. They did much together until December when Jenny's focus turned to the return of John. She had saved all his letters, read them, and reread them, and he would be home for Christmas break in a few days.

The day he arrived, she knew he was home because she had been in town and seen the carriage go through. Finishing work the next day, she went to their spot in the glen; they had agreed to meet at 6:00 PM. She arrived at 5:30 PM. She felt the familiar stirrings of excitement. It was as if her whole body was smiling. She listened for the familiar clop, clop, clop of his horse. That sound never came; John never came. With tears rolling down her cheeks, Jenny turned and started for home. Where was he? He must have met someone else. She realized that this would happen one day, and perhaps it had, but why hadn't he told her? She looked up, searching for Smailholm Tower directly behind Walter Scott's house. That tower was so high you could see it throughout the valley; however, now the clouds completely covered the tower. 'Strange,' thought Jenny, 'the sky is clear here, but the tower is blanketed with fog.' Looking at the clouds again, she began to comprehend that they were much blacker than normal and rolling straight upwards. 'Oh my, oh my, those are not clouds; that is smoke!' "Oh my God!" she screamed "John's house is on fire!" Racing back toward her house, she sprinted into the barn and jumped on her horse,

Bay. Da was working in the shop; he looked up startled and asked, "What's wrong? Where are you going?"

"Fire, I think, fire at the Scotts!" With that, she raced down the dirt path toward John. She rode Bay across the path through the stiff heather, and as they rounded the curve, she saw the flames licking out like blistering tongues flickering out through the black smoke. "My God, John, please be safe. God, please let him be safe," she prayed. She arrived at the gate to see Walter Scott's workers pulling the fire wagon out. She jumped off Bay and ran to help. "Have you seen John?" she shouted to one of the men. "He is supposed to be here!"

"I haven't seen him."

"You haven't...my God, he must be inside!" Jenny let go of the wagon and began running toward the door. One of the men sprinted after her and caught her just before she reached the door.

"No, you can't go in there, miss. It is too dangerous."

"What is going on?" Thomas Dodds shouted as he rode up and saw that Sam McNairy was holding onto Jenny.

"Da, John is in there."

"John?" He looked at her questioningly but ran toward the house.

"Wait, Thomas," Sam yelled. "Let me do it! Doug, bring the ax over here!" Doug brought a bucket of water and the ax and handed it to Sam who ran past Thomas. He smashed the door with the ax and stepped back, expecting flames to shoot out from the opening. There were no flames. Sam felt the door. It was warm, not hot. He opened the door and stepped back again.

"No flames," Thomas said as he peered in. Jenny was right behind him.

"John, John, where are you?" Her heart was racing. Breathing stopped as she saw the flames gobbling up everything inside.

"Get her out of here!" Doug yelled to Thomas. Thomas grabbed his daughter by the arm, pulling her away from the house, wondering for a moment why she was so upset. "Jenny, the fire is not that bad. It is not coming out the windows, and why are you yelling for John Scott?" As soon as he said it, he knew. "Oh, girl, I see. You fancy the boy." He had no time to go on because the men came over with the good news that the flames were out. The large rug in front of the fireplace had caught an ember, and before it was put out, fire had destroyed the draperies and the large buffet.

Jenny broke away from her father, never answering his question, racing up the stairs taking two at a time. John was not in his room or anywhere upstairs. She ran back down the stairs in a panic. Arriving home from shopping, Charles, the butler, was dumbfounded by the activity he faced. Before he could get in the door, Jenny was asking about John. Charles had no word on when John was arriving for his break, but he told her John was not there.

Seeing that everything was under control, Thomas mounted his horse and pulled Bay over for Jenny to mount. "Come on, Lass, we have some talking to do." And so it was that Thomas Dodds discovered that John and Jenny were more than friends or acquaintances. Thomas reminded his daughter, "You know nothing can come of it. He cannot take you for his wife."

"I know, but Da, I love him, and he loves me."

"Then why wasn't he there to meet you, Jen?" She had no answer for him, but she could not believe that he would do this to her on purpose. He must have had a reason.

"Better stick with your own kind, Lass; nothing going to come of it but hurt." Thomas patted Jenny on the back.

"Are you going to tell Ma?"

"Oh, no, not me. You are telling her, Jenny." Telling came that night after supper. Helen was not surprised because she had seen them talking at last summer's fair. She had left it alone since there was no sign of inappropriate behavior. Later, Helen and Thomas talked and decided that it was an infatuation and would fade with time. Besides, the young man was gone most of the year, but Fergus was here. "We'll watch and see, but I'm sure she will come to her senses soon, and if not, we are leaving in the spring so that will settle the matter," Thomas assured his wife.

Jenny was distraught. She sobbed her eyes out at their special place under the alders. On one of those days, her mother followed her. She held her to her breast as she had when Jenny was a young girl. "Jenny, you will get through this. There will be another."

"No, I don't want another, and I am not upset thinking he doesn't want to see me; I am upset because something is wrong, bad wrong. I know he wouldn't do this to me. He is just not like that, Ma. I know him."

Helen's heart went out to her oldest daughter. She did not know John Scott, though she did know young men and that in the hands of the young, love can be cruel. Secretly, she hoped that John had come to his senses and walked away from Jenny. Fergus Walton was an excellent choice for her daughter. He was stable and would support his family and be a good husband to her.

Gail Huntley

Chapter VIII

The last time Jenny visited their meeting place, the alder trees resembled white reindeer antlers jutting out from the snow banked up against their crooked trunks, stark statues against the gray sky. Eight-year-old Mary ran alongside Jenny, jumping up and catching snowflakes with her tongue. "Jenny, what do you want for Christmas this year?"

"Oh, I don't know."

"You don't know. Well, I do. I want pipes."

"What? Pipes? You want a bagpipe?" Jenny asked, surprised by Mary's wish because girls did not play the pipes.

"Yes, Da let me blow his once, and now I want my own." Thomas played the bagpipes at all the local functions. He had inherited his pipes from his great-great-grandfather who was a famous piper throughout the highlands. He had moved to the borders after losing his land to the fierce Gordon clan. Ironically, many years later, his granddaughter and grandson married into the Gordon and Stewart clans. Consequently, though he had lost his land, he had saved his family and his pipes.

"Well, little one, you never know what can happen at Christmastime. It is a magical time, but Mary, not a word to anyone about Christmas. Remember, we cannot celebrate." Jenny put her fingers to her lips, "Shhh." The Presbyterian Church had banned Christmas celebrations for years; however, several families, including the Doddses, did celebrate with small tree displays, a gift for each child, and a special dinner when they could afford such luxuries.

"I know; I won't tell, Jenny. You know I never do."

"I know, little one," Jenny replied picking her up and spinning her around in a circle; Jenny wondered if Da knew Mary wanted to play the pipes. Of course, they could not afford to buy her this instrument, but she knew Da and Ma would laugh over this unusual request from their youngest daughter.

"She wants a bagpipe?" Helen said incredulously.

"Yes. She is musically inclined."

"I know," her mother said; "she picks at the piano at church and can actually play some hymns, but pipes?"

"And that voice too," Thomas remarked. "Did you tell her she would not get bagpipes for Christmas?"

"No, Da; I couldn't."

"I understand. I will talk with her," Helen said, shaking her head as she turned to gather up the breakfast dishes. "Bagpipes ... my goodness. Imagine, a girl playing bagpipes."

Jenny asked her father, "can't she play yours?"

"No, I wish she could, but with the extra income they bring in, I can't afford to let her use them. Besides, they are too big for her."

"Oh; well, maybe you could whittle her a horn, Da," Tom Jr. said in jest.

"That is a promising idea, Tom."

"I wasn't serious, Da, you don't think...."

"Oh, but maybe, just maybe," he said as the wheels began whirring, conjuring up an idea in his head. Soon he had his hat and coat on and disappeared out the door.

Jenny interrupted her mother's thoughts by saying, "Ma, do you realize that this will be the last Christmas we spend in this house?" She looked at the large old clock her grandfather had made that sat on the mantle above the fire. He had carved a roan's head and antlers at the top. The antlers reached out halfway to the ceiling. On both sides of the mahogany clock, he had carved a long-stemmed thistle. The clock sat above the beautiful mahogany table Thomas had built. She thought, 'I was born here. I have laid my head down on my box bed every day of my life. I love this house. I love Scotland' and then she said "Ma, I don't want to leave."

"I know, none of us does."

"That is for sure," Tom remarked.

"I'm serious. I am not a child anymore. I can stay."

"You can, if you marry. You can't stay without a husband."

"Why can't I?"

"Because you cannot protect yourself or own or rent land. You know that, Jenny, or are you thinking of marrying the Walton boy?"

"No and yes. I have thought about it. I guess I would have to marry to stay unless I could live with Grandpa and grandma Rule in Jedburgh." There, it was said, never to be taken back.

"What?" Ann gasped as she jumped up from the game she was playing with her sister.

Helen took a breath. She was not expecting this. It had never occurred to her that not all the children would want to go with them. She turned, wiped her hands on her apron, and told Jenny to sit down. Tom, Ann, Robert, and Mary gathered around, each of them feeling the loss of their big sister already. George started to cry and curled up on Jenny's lap.

Finding her voice, Helen looked at Jenny and choosing her words carefully said, "Well, Jenny, that is a big decision, and you would have to ask your father and your grandparents about that, but we really want you to be with us. You know that once we leave, we will never return, and you will probably never see us again."

"I know, and that is why the decision is so hard." She looked down at her little sister who was now pleading with her not to leave them. A single tear welled up in Jenny's eye and trailed down her cheek. She loved her family. She would die for them. However, she would also die for the man hidden deep in her heart that she would never see again if she went to America. As hard as she tried, she could not dampen that little flame of hope that still burned in her heart even though it had been months now with no word from him or his uncle.

Jenny continued to go to SandyKnowe, but no one was there except Charles, and he had no news. After a while, Jenny realized that Charles would share no news. He was loyal, and butlers did not disclose information about their employers. She began to understand that John did not want her or was choosing to stay away from her. She knew she must move on, so taking her mother's advice, she began seeing Fergus Walton. She attended the fall dance with Fergus and asked him to come for Christmas supper. He was a good man, but try as she might, she could not stop thinking about John Scott. She continued to ask Lucille about letters, but none had arrived. She watched for Uncle Walter to come home, but he had not.

Christmas Eve rolled in with a horrendous blizzard. The women were busy in the kitchen baking. Five-year-old George was playing with the popcorn strings that were to go on the little scotch pine tree they had cut down and brought in. Thomas and Ann were gathering the last of the sheep before the storm hit the hardest, and Robert was hunting pheasant for Christmas dinner.

Cresting the hill above Coulter's silo, Robert caught sight of a colorful bird perched in the snow underneath a giant oak tree. There was his pheasant for Christmas dinner! The ground was covered in a thin layer of snow with leftover heather poking through. The pheasant continued to peck at the seeds it had found under the tree. Robert smiled, knowing it would be an easy shot. He lifted his shotgun to his shoulder and squeezed the trigger. Suddenly, before he completed the trigger pull, a shot rang out and echoed through the mountain air. Robert lowered his gun and watched as a man dressed in black watch plaid from head to toe came out of the patch of trees east of Robert. The man walked over and picked up the bird.

"Hey, ho!" Robert shouted as he began to run down the hill. "You shot my pheasant!"

The man turned and looked at Robert. "What?"

"You shot my bird. I had my sights on him."

"Well, sorry, Laddie, but it appears that you were a little too late. I already shot him, see?" He held up the bird.

Frustrated, Robert replied, "I see that, but what I'm saying is he should have been mine."

"And how would I know that, Lad? Am I to be a mind reader? I didn't see you there, Laddie, and if you'd been a whisker sooner he would be yours. Hmm, you look like one of the Doddses. What's your name, Lad?"

"I am Robert, Robert Dodds."

"Oh, yes, yes. You are Jenny's brother, right?"

"Uh, yes." Finally, Robert recognized the man. It was Mr. Walter Scott. "When did you return? We haven't seen you in a long time."

"Well, I was away, but now I'm back. Oh, by the way, would you tell your sister to come on box day (the day after Christmas)? I have some family here, and the house will need a cleaning."

"Yes, I will tell her." Robert, knowing how Jenny had been grieving for John, asked, "Is John there?"

"Yes, yes, he is; guess you heard that we almost lost him. He's been sick, bad sick, poor lad. Polio got him, and he is just recovering enough to come see his old uncle. Has your sister been looking for him?"

"Oh my, that is terrible about John. Yes, yes, Jenny is doling around like someone died, but how do you know about them?"

"Oh, I know things, especially things about love and young ones. Tell her to come if she likes, but he cannot go out for extended periods yet."

Robert was elated to hear the news about John. Not that he had polio but that he was recovering from it. "I will. I will tell her. She will be so happy. But now I must get myself a pheasant for our dinner."

"I'll tell you what, I already got one in here (he pointed to his pack basket), so you can have this one if you are a mind to."

"Oh no, I couldn't; it is yours."

"Son, you had better take it and get home. Look down there." Walter pointed in the direction of the Doddses' farm, and Robert saw the solid block of white forming just past the stone wall of the river. "We got us a blizzard coming. Come on; get on my old horse here, and we'll get you home quickly." Walter handed the pheasant to Robert who climbed on the back of the horse, and they began their descent into the valley. Soon, even the large pines were hidden by the wall of white.

"How can you see, Sir?" Robert shouted into the wind.

"Oh, Laddie, I've been coming here since I was just a boy. I know every inch of this land. I know every tree, every rock, and every pretty lassie that dwells here." With that, he chuckled, and Robert smiled. He liked this man who talked too much and gave him a pheasant for Christmas. By the time they reached the farm, the snow was coming down faster than a windmill spinning in a storm.

"Sir, you'd better stay with us."

"Nah," he patted his horse on the neck, "this old horse knows her way home, but I see the path through the glen is filling fast with snow, so I must leave you now and wander on home. I'll be there in no time. Thank you, anyway." Robert watched him leave. Within seconds, the black watch jacket and hat had disappeared. Yes, Mr. Scott had been traveling that path for many years, so he would make it home just as he always had done. Seeing this man wandering through the countryside in all kinds of weather was not a shock to the folks who lived in border country. Robert turned and hurried into the little cottage to show his ma what he had shot and to tell Jenny the news about John.

Helen had begun to worry about Robert and Thomas. Neither of them was home. Thomas had returned in the morning with Ann and disappeared again not saying anything to anyone. Fergus had arrived an hour before covered in snow relating how fast the snow was coming down. Jenny took his coat and brought him to Da's chair by the fire to thaw out.

Just as Helen was about to send Tom out to check on his brother, Robert burst through the thick wood door holding up a large pheasant, "Look what I got, Ma!" he shouted lifting the bird Walter had given him. He reasoned that there was no need to tell who had shot the bird because if Mr. Scott had not been there, Robert would not have missed.

"Good job, Robert. That looks like a nice fat one. It will make an extra special Christmas dinner." Helen had mutton ready for dinner in case there was no bird, but pheasant was another tradition carried on in

78

the Dodds household on the forbidden Christmas Day, so Helen was pleased, although she was still worrying about her husband's disappearance. She could hear the wind howling through the valley and hoped he wasn't out in the field somewhere. "Ma, I'm going to see if I can see him from the porch," Jenny said as she buttoned her coat and pulled her wool stocking cap over her head.

"Jenny, just look. Do not go anywhere in this storm!" Helen shouted as Jen slid the latch on the thick wooden door. It blew open pushing her back.

Fergus jumped up, "Jenny, wait. Let me go." He grabbed his coat and hat, raced to her, shut the door, and secured the latch before everything blew away. Jenny began to remove the latch again and this time Fergus held the door while they stepped out on the porch. They both pulled the door shut. Standing on the porch was difficult. The wind was so strong that she had to hang onto the post. Jenny hollered into the wind, but she knew that even if her father was close by he would not hear her. Just as they were ready to come back in, grandfather came out the door. Grandfather and Grandmother Dodds had come the day before, which was another Christmas tradition.

"Is there a light in the barn?" They both looked. There was no light. The only sound was the whistle of the wind through the hills. Snow continued falling silently all around them. "Well, I think we better check," Grandpa said. "Come inside a minute." They went inside, and Grandpa went to the drawer in the sideboard and returned with a rope. "I am going to tie this to the door handle and follow it out to the barn. Jenny, you stay by the door."

Tom saw what Grandpa was doing and rushed over, "No, Grandpa, I've got this."

"Laddie, I am fine; I can do this."

Grandma spoke up, "You may be fine, you old Scotsman, but Tom is young and strong. Let him do it."

"Grandpa, why don't you stay by the door. I will go. Keep the line taunt. If I get lost, I will return. When I get to the barn, I will light the lantern and wave it outside. I will wave it twice if all is well and three times if I need help. If I need help, send Robert and Fergus. I will tie the rope to the barn door, so we have a way back." They all agreed on that plan, so Tom began wading through the thigh-high snow toward a barn he could not see. He gauged his direction by the tall pine trees he could still see in the shadows. After struggling for what Tom judged to be about fifty feet, he still could not see the barn. The wind screamed and tugged at Tom's hat. He was glad he had latched the buckle under his chin, so the wool earflaps stayed snug. His muscles ached as he pushed into the snow with his body. The further out he traveled, the higher the snow was on his body, and he was now using his whole body to make a path. The snow was up to his hips. He held tight to the rope knowing that if he lost his grip, he could be lost forever in this blizzard. When he pulled one foot out of the sucking snow, the hole it had created immediately filled in. Several times the sheer force of the wind slammed him down so he was sitting on the snow. He knew that the barn should be directly in front of him now. He stopped and looked straight ahead where the barn should be. It was not. A branch flew within inches of his face, and the snow pelted his skin feeling like tiny pebbles hitting his face. Looking ahead and just to the right side of his hips Tom saw something black protruding out of the snow. He brushed it off with his glove. It was the rock! This was the old rock he had played on since he could walk. He knew where he was! He turned left and struggled in the snow, continuing to make a path with his body. After four steps, he saw the shadow of the barn looming above him. Three more steps, and he was at the door. He turned back toward the house and waved the lantern two times. He took off his gloves and tied the rope to the door handle then lifted the latch, slid the door to the left, and stepped in. "Da, you in here?" he called. All was silent except the howling wind. 'Maybe he is in his shop,' Tom thought, though that seemed strange given the weather and that it was Christmas Eve. He called several more times as he headed toward the shop door. He looked down and saw a flickering yellow light. 'Oh my God, fire,' he thought. "Da, Da!" he shouted as he ran toward the door.

Suddenly, the door opened. "What is it, Tom? Is something wrong?"

"Yes, something is wrong, Da. You are missing."

"What? Missing. Why I've been right here."

"But what is that light? Is there a fire?"

"What light? Oh, this?" Thomas opened the door. The bright light hit Tom in the face. Putting his hand over his eyes, he looked around the room. He saw four lanterns lit in the little six-by-eight-foot room.

"Da, why do you have so many lanterns lit?"

"In order to see my whittling."

"Whittling?"

"Yes, well the secret is out so come and see what I am making for your sister." Thomas picked up a beautiful shiny object. "She wanted bagpipes, but as you know we cannot afford that, so I made her this." Tom was amazed when he looked at this wood pipe with the tiny holes his father had carved down the front and one in the back for her thumb. Da had polished it until the wood gleamed. "Listen, Tom." Thomas put the instrument up to his mouth, blew into it, moved his fingers, and created a beautiful mellow sound.

Tom beamed with pride for this wonderful creative man that was his da. "It is like the pipe without the bag."

"Yes, I hope she is not too sad about not getting the bagpipe."

"She will love it, but how long have you been out here?"

"Most of the day. I wanted to finish it tonight."

"We have been looking for you because there is a terrible blizzard. Come with me." Tom brought Thomas to the door and opened it.

"Oh, my Lord! It was snowing a bit when I came out here this morning, but I had no idea." There were no windows in the shop, and when Thomas became interested in something, he could focus intently for hours forgetting everything else.

"I have a rope tethered from the barn to the house," Tom related. This was not the first time they had had to connect the cottage to the barn. Snow or no snow, animals had to be fed and milked, and hay had to be put up.

"Good, and the gift is finished, so let me put it in the box I have for it, and we will make our way to the house." He put the pipe in the box, wrapped it with burlap and put it inside his coat. Then they doused the lights and grabbed tightly onto the rope, Thomas leading the way as the two of them braced the snow and wind on the trek back to the house. Grandpa, Jenny, and Fergus were still out on the porch watching for them, and everyone cheered to see Da in the doorway. He received a good scolding from Helen about not telling anyone where he was going. He apologized for breaking his own rule and vowed he would never do it again.

Finally, even before Jen took off her coat, Robert was beckoning her to come to the loft. She climbed the stairs and said, "God, Robert, what is so important? I have to help Ma with supper."

The words flew out of his mouth, "I've news about John."

"Oh my God," her hands flew to her mouth. Her throat tightened and breathing stopped.

"I met his Uncle Walter while I was hunting. He told me that John has been sick. Jenny, he has polio."

"No, oh Lord, is he; is he?"

"He is recovering, and he was well enough to come to SandyKnowe."

"He's here!" Jenny screeched in disbelief, covering her mouth when she realized the family might hear.

"Yes. He wants to see you."

"Oh yes, oh yes. I want to go right now. Oh, thank you, Robert. This is the best Christmas present ever." She hugged him.

"Okay, okay," Robert said pulling out of her grasp, "but you can't go tonight. We are having dinner, and it is still snowing out there. Besides, Mr. Scott wants you to come clean on the day after Christmas."

"Oh, yes, oh thank you Robert. This is the best Christmas present ever."

By Christmas morning the winds had calmed, and Little Mary's squeals of delight could be heard by all as she opened the box under the tree, and then the squeals of the pipe could be heard by all until Helen finally told her she needed to put it down so they could have a little quiet on this joyful day of the savior's birth.

They ate the pheasant that day, and Jenny was bursting with joy though it was clouded by having to wait until tomorrow to see John. Adding to her problems was Fergus Walton who was spending another night, which meant that he would be there in the morning before Jenny went to work at the Scott manor. She knew he would offer to take her in his sleigh and her parents would expect her to go with him. Jenny became quiet as she glared out the window at the storm. John was home, and now this. John was home. She must focus on that, and so she did. Helen and Thomas thought her unusual joy was due to Christmas and Fergus being by her side. She had moved past her infatuation with John Scott and was falling for Fergus, they thought.

"Jenny, Jenny," Fergus chided as he tried to get her attention. They had finished supper and the dishes were put away. Everyone except the two had retired for the night. Jenny had made a bed for Fergus on the floor in front of the fireplace, and the two sat on the feather pillows drinking tea and watching the flames dance. Jenny's thoughts were still on a plan for tomorrow.

"Jenny?"

"Oh, Fergus, sorry. Yes, what is it?"

"My, my, you were lost in thought. Thinking about the move?"

"Uh, the move. Oh yes, yes; the move." She turned her face to Fergus, "I am sorry, Fergus, I am not very good company, I guess. Did you enjoy the supper and celebrating Christmas with us?" Fergus had never celebrated Christmas before this year.

"Oh, yes, and I think we need to talk, Jenny."

"We do?"

"Yes, Lass, I did so enjoy Christmas with you and would love to enjoy many more. I know you are trying to decide whether to leave for America in the spring, and I have an idea that may help you with that decision."

"An idea. Okay."

"I am in love with you. I always have been, and I have a trade that I can do anywhere. I would like to marry you. I am willing to live here or get on a ship and go to America with you. It would be your choice. Jenny Dodds, will you marry me?" He bent down on one knee, took a box out of his pocket, and held it out for Jenny to see. It was a beautiful diamond ring, ironically, the one she had seen at Mr. Tucker's jewelry store a couple of weeks before when she and Fergus had gone in to look at watches for his father. She had toyed with the fantasy of John giving her this ring. She liked it because the tiny stone matched the blue of John's eyes. 'Heavens,' she thought, 'what am I to do, now?'

"Well?"

"Ah…."

"Jenny, please. I don't mean to rush you." Fergus stood up and sat back down next to her. He took her hand. "I know you weren't expecting this, but decisions must be made because of the trip. If you stay here, you need a husband, and I would like that to be me. I will always be here for you."

"Oh my, Fergus, I am flattered."

"Jenny, I know you are not in love with me, but you are fond of me, aren't you?"

"I am. Of course, I am, but fondness is not enough for marriage."

"I believe your feelings will grow for me because I will be so good to you. You don't have to answer me now. You can think about it. I know it is a big decision."

"Oh, Fergus, you are so kind, but I still haven't decided if I will go with my family, and you said you could never leave Scotland."

"I know, but some things are worth moving across the world for."

"You are such a good man, but I can't say yes right now. I don't know what I want."

She saw the hurt in his face. She watched him put that beautiful ring back in his pocket. "Fergus, just give me some time, please."

He looked up and smiled, a smile that lit up his face and made his brown eyes sparkle, "That I can do, my love; that I can do."

Feeling restless and guilty, she bid Fergus good night, climbed up the ladder, and got into her bed. Her two sisters were already asleep. The house was silent as snow, and sleep did not come to Jenny Dodds.

Gail Huntley

CHAPTER IX

The next morning, Jenny was the first one up. She peered out the small window and saw the white snow glistening like diamonds in the morning sun. This was a rarity for a Scottish border winter. 'It is a sign from God that John and I are to be together,' she thought. She remembered in the middle of the night that Walter Scott had told Robert to have her come the day after Christmas, and here it was. At breakfast, she related that she had to clean the Scott house. This was another sign that it was meant to be. She did not even need a plan. Sir Walter gave her the excuse to see John. Of course, her father asked Fergus to take her if the snow stopped. If not, she was not to go until it was safe. She opened the door and looked out. Ah, yes, it was safe. The snow had stopped in the night.

"Fergus, we have to go now. The snow has stopped," said Jenny. She felt a twinge of guilt that this man who loved her would be bringing her into the arms of another. It was not that Jenny did not give serious thought to Fergus' proposal; she did. It was sound, and her parents approved of him. He would be a good provider, husband, and father, which was not always the case among young Scottish men. Some were brutes who spent more time in the pubs than with their families; poverty had hardened some, and a few were good solid marrying men. Jenny's problem right now was that she could not force her head to rule her heart. She also knew that John could never be her husband. Soon he would marry a woman chosen by his parents and produce heirs to the Scott dynasty. Jenny was a practical girl, and she thought maybe eventually her common sense would win over her emotions, but now was not the time. She needed to make sure John was okay, and then she could come back and think about Fergus, his proposal, and the move.

"Okay, Jen, Fergus replied, I'll go get the horse hooked up."

"I'll help," Jenny quickly replied. Soon they were dressed and out the door. Finally, through much effort, they made it out to the barn, saddled the dray horse, hooked up the cart, and began their trek down the snow-laden trail. Jenny watched Jake, the big workhorse stepping high over the white blanket of snow that surrounded them. She wondered if they would have to turn back, but it was a light fluffy snow, and soon Jake was trotting along effortlessly kicking out the snow in front of him. The trees glistened bright in the morning sun, and Jenny's thoughts traveled to her conversation with her father about moving. She wrapped her brown scarf around her face to protect it against the chilly wind blowing across the fields. Fergus had thrown a sheepskin blanket over their laps, and that helped keep out the dampness. Gently falling snowflakes came in for a soft landing on the sleeves of the new blue cape her mother had made her for Christmas. How could she move from here, this beautiful place she loved: magically white in the winter, purple heather in the September hills peppered with craggy tree trunks, and fast-flowing waters that ushered in the spring thaw? "Fergus, seriously, could you ever move from here?"

"You mean out of Scotland?"

"Yes."

"I told you I would."

"You know, Ma and Da are definitely going to America."

"No turning back, then. It is for sure."

"I believe so, Fergus."

"And you will go? Have you decided?"

"I don't want to, Fergus. I don't want to leave my home, but I may have to."

"No, sweet, that's what I am saying; you won't have to if you marry me, Jenny. I can take care of you."

"I know, Fergus. It's just...."

"Just what?"

"Well, you know I would never see them again. My whole family would be out of my life forever."

"Forever is a long time, Jenny girl."

"Yes, it is." Tears filled her eyes, and she looked away. Fergus took her hand, and they continued the ride in silence in their own thoughts about the ramifications of her impending journey.

When they reached the top of the hill right before Scott manor, Fergus stopped the horse and turned to Jenny. "You know, Lass, I repeat: if you want to go, I will go with you. I heard you can own your own land there. I could do that. We are young and strong, and we could help your parents until we buy our own land. Your father said that settlers can get their own land by working for a landowner for two years and paying a little each month. But Jeff Rutherford told me that not too far from where your father will settle is a mountainous place off a large lake called Lake Champlain where there is free land. You get fifty acres free and then each acre beyond that is very cheap. He lives in a settlement called Chestertown."

"My, my, Fergus, you have been studying this, haven't you, but fifty acres free! Come on, Fergus, that has got to be a tall tale." Jenny knew Jeff Rutherford. He had left with his parents last year. He and Fergus were friends, but she did not know he had heard from him.

"So, you have heard from Jeff?"

"Yes, he sent me one letter, but I haven't heard from him since."

"Did he say anything about his family?"

"Not much except they were well and had settled in a place called Maine near the ocean instead of where Jeff is. Mrs. Rutherford had a sister and brother-in-law there, so they all moved to Maine. However, Jeff left and found this place in New York he liked. You know Jeff, a man of his own with many spoken words and few written words. Jen, listen to me. You and I, we get on so well together, and I think you would come to love me."

"Oh, Fergus, I am so flattered that you would leave your family and country for me, but I told you, I need time to think this through."

"I know. I'm sorry, and you shall have your time, my love; I will not broach this subject again. It will have to come from you."

"Thank you, Fergus." Jenny reached up and hugged him. "But, we must move on. I have plenty of work to do for the Scotts today. We can talk about this another time."

"Oh, yes, of course we can; off we go then." He pulled on the reins, and the old horse began the last few yards up over the ridge and down the hill to the mammoth stone mansion. Five minutes later, they pulled up in front of the two pillars standing guard on each side of the walkway. "When do you want me to pick you up?"

"You don't need...."

"No, Jenny, your father told me to pick you up, too."

"I was just going to say that the Scotts' driver takes me home sometimes."

"Not today, though. What time?"

"Uh, okay, Fergus. Pick me up at 5:00 PM."

"Okay, I'll be here. Bye, then."

"Bye." Jenny turned and raced up the steps to the wide front door. She lifted her arm and reached out for the lion head doorknocker when she heard a tapping sound above her. She looked up. There he was in the window waving at her. The mere image of him in the window took her breath away. She quickly grabbed the knocker and within minutes, Charles opened the door.

Charles greeted her with his usual stiff body bow and "Miss Dodds," took her coat and muff, and with a twinkle in his eye told her that Master John was upstairs in his room. Jenny ran up the stairs taking two at time. She knocked on the door.

"Come in, Jenny," John said. At first, she could not hear him, so she knocked a second time, opened the door a crack, and saw him sitting up in bed. He motioned her in. Sitting before her was a man half the size he had been when she had last seen him. It shocked her into silence. His face was as white as the snow outside the window, and his speech was barely above a whisper. "I know; I know. I look like the ghost from hell, but it is me."

Struggling to breathe, Jenny stuttered, "No, no, John; you look fine." She stood before him pulling on her fingers not knowing what to do. His face was hollowed out as if he were sucking in his cheeks. Red circles rimmed his beautiful blue eyes. The only remnant of John was his thick blond hair that still flowed in waves down to his shoulders.

"Well, Lassie, you should have seen me when I was sick," he said with a weak smile. "Come over here and give me a hug. I won't break."

With those words, Jenny ran to his bedside, sat on the bed, leaned over, and hugged him. "Oh John, I've missed you so much. I was so worried. I had no idea you were sick. Robert saw your uncle on a hunt, and he told him."

"I know, and I am sorry. I thought about you many times, but I was too sick to write and Ma and Da took care of me. Seriously, Jenny, I know I look bad, but I am much better. As soon as they let me, I made the trip here. I made the trip to see you. I knew you would come to clean after Christmas. I couldn't contact you at your house, of course, and then the storm."

"John, I don't care. I am just so glad you are here." Jenny leaned over, and they kissed for the first time in months. He pulled her down on top of him. She had no will to stop him, and soon their kisses carried them off to a place Jenny had never been before. She rolled over beside him, and they stared into each other's eyes. She could not help herself. She had missed him with every fiber of her being, and now every fiber was on fire. "John, I love you. I love you more than ever. Can we? Can you?"

John looked at her. "Oh my God, my sweet Jenny, I love you too, and yes I can. Are you sure?"

"I am surer of this than I have ever been of anything." She took his hand and put it to her breast.

"Oh Lord, Lassie, you feel so good" he whispered, as he began unbuttoning her dress, and on that snowy morning in that bed with the love of her life, Jenny Dodds became a woman.

When it was over, Jenny rested her head on his chest reliving every moment until John fell asleep. She slid off the bed, kissed him on the cheek, and went downstairs to do her chores. All day, she felt like she was floating. She could not help but smile at anything, such as the ray of sun coming in through the window or Uncle Walter's Irish setter that flopped about the house. Dusting and mopping had never been such joyous tasks; she could feel her lover's presence throughout the house. Later she would bring him hot soup and make sure he was warm. Now when they looked at each other, there was a knowing, a knowing shared by only the two of them. "Jenny, are you sorry?"

"Oh, no my love. I am happy. I just wish…."

"I know. Me too." They knew. She lay down beside him. He put his arm under her head. She rolled over and lay the side of her cheek on his chest. She could hear the rattle still plaguing him, and it unnerved her. She did not want to say anything to spoil what they had, so she moved her head to the crook of his arm and relished the last few minutes they had together. She wanted this moment to last forever, to stay in his arms for eternity. Tears filled her eyes as her senses overtook her emotions and the reality of their situation broke through.

"Don't cry, Jenny," John whispered. "We must be happy with what we have. We are present, and now there is love all around us. Don't you feel it?"

Jenny wiped the tears from her eyes and smiled, "Oh, yes, I do, and I hear your uncle's words in you."

"Ah, I am a romantic, my love, but so much more when I have you in my arms." He kissed her one more time before they heard the knock on the door.

"Miss Jenny, your ride is here."

CHAPTER X

As winter waned, the Doddses' home became a flurry of excitement with villagers coming to get the real news about their impending voyage. Robert and Ann were now excited, telling their friends how they would be living among the trees and learning to shoot a bow and arrow like those Indians over there. Jenny and Helen Dodds were not that enthusiastic. Helen had heard and read tales of passengers getting small pox, dysentery, and other deadly illnesses. She heard stories of ships lost forever in vicious sea storms. Even if the ocean voyage went well, what would they encounter once they landed on the stark Newfoundland shores? The newspapers carried articles about Indians, fierce storms, and dangerous animals in America.

To add to the negative thoughts, Helen wondered how they would fare with their only relative being a horse thief. Perhaps, she thought, they don't even know about Uncle Wright Rule's thievery in Scotland. She guessed that could be a good thing. He was also a clever, resourceful man, though it may be with other people's resources. She smiled to herself as she recalled his mischievous blue eyes and the laughter he brought into the house when he burst through the door, larger than life, with some new adventure to tell about. As unconventional a man as he was, the family never believed he was going to America, but he did, and now they would be setting their trust in him. Helen tried to warn her husband about her father's brother, but she did not think Thomas understood that the dynamic, loving, jolly family man Thomas knew could also be untrustworthy, conniving, and likely to pick up his hat and move on whenever the notion hit him. Helen wondered if he would even be there when they arrived. Thomas trusted him, so she surrendered her initial protests about settling near Uncle Wright and Aunt Catherine who lived in Rossie, New York.

On March 2, 1819, Thomas Dodds set out for town to visit the weaver and clerk of the kirk session, William Hamilton, who would transcribe for Thomas the baptismal entries of his six children. Thomas was not a man to leave anything to chance, and now that he had Helen's approval, he went ahead with the arrangements to set sail. William Hamilton was one of Thomas' closest friends. He was not happy to see him go. "Thomas, are you sure you want to do this? It is so far and quite dangerous."

"I know, Will, but I hardly have a choice. I'm losing my job. I know it. If I don't give notice, Laird Buccleuch will have to let me go anyway. Several other tenants have already packed up and gone. You of all people know that these large manor houses can no longer sustain the grandeur that once was. That way of life is leaving us and with it the farmers who keep it running."

"Right, Thomas, but with your carpentry skills you could stay in Scotland and earn a wage."

"Yes, I could, barely getting by. We hardly get by now with the farm and my extra work. No, Will, I've made up my mind; I'm going to America. Now, can you have those papers ready for me the first part of next month?"

"Yes, my friend, they will be ready." Thomas walked out into the dusty street just missing Donald McNab's horse as the cart recklessly careened around the corner square.

"Hey, slow that thing down, Lad!" he yelled, waving his fist at the boy. Donald glanced back and kept on going. "Young lads always in a hurry," Thomas muttered as he brushed off his pants now covered in dirt. He climbed on his horse and trotted through his town. The large gray stones of the village square were still there along with the little white church he had grown up in. He would never see this again. He knew it. There would never be enough money or time to return. A sadness covered his heart, and tears sprang from his eyes as he rode Ginger, his horse, over the mossy glen and through the green valley where he had walked hand and hand with Helen so many years ago. They had married in that church. He turned and gazed back over the hills across SandyKnowe where the great tower scraped the sky. Next month would be the last time his eyes would take in this magnificent sight.

Plodding along, Thomas gazed at the flax fields stretched as far as he could see on both sides of the road now brown with fertile land waiting for spring when they would erupt into a blanket of blue for miles and miles. He would be gone before they bloomed this year. In the distance, Thomas saw a flock of sheep trotting down the road followed by the shepherd's dog and then the shepherd sauntering along smoking his pipe. Thomas moved into the field allowing them to pass by. "Good day to you," said Thomas. He did not recognize the shepherd, but he knew the sheep had once belonged to the Rutherfords. He wondered if they had felt such sorrow when they were ready to leave. He hoped he would be able to find them in America.

During his last months in Scotland, Thomas took a large quantity of yarn to his friend, Hamilton, who was also a weaver, and had him weave 70 yards of shirting, 96 yards of blankets, and 55 yards of sheeting. As a side business, Thomas ran a 'jenny a' thing,' a shop that carries religious merchandise. Though he took some of these items on the voyage, he sold many of them to pay off his debts and raise money.

Figure 2. Lessudden Main Street.

On April 5, 1819, Thomas paid his weaving bill in full, and the next day Hamilton issued the baptismal certificates of the children.

Tom Jr. greeted his father when he arrived home and he asked, "Da, did you get the papers?"

"Sure did, Lad. We are ready." He walked over to his son who had a pitchfork in his hand and was putting fresh straw out for the horses. "Da, is it true that we can own our land there?"

"That's what your uncle says and a few others I've talked to."

"You know what, cousin James told me that you can vote there even if you are a farmer."

"Oh, he did, did he? Where did you see him?"

"At SandyKnowe. He is teaching that young John Scott his lessons because John is sick. Jenny said she didn't like him, but I understand he writes poetry and he and Mr. Scott are friends. Da, you know Jenny might not go, don't you?"

Thomas stared down at his son. "What? No, I did not know. I just assumed she was since she had not said she was not. I guess that means she will be wedding Fergus Walton."

"Uh, I don't think so; uh, don't know. Maybe. Guess you'll have to ask her," Tom stammered as he jammed the fork into the mound of hay in corner of the barn.

"Well, she'd better be making up her mind soon. Tomorrow is the last day I can cancel her ticket and get my money back," Thomas said as he shook his head, put his arm over his son's shoulders, and walked toward the house. He had a mind to order her to go with them whether she said yes to Fergus or not. He could not bring himself to think about never seeing her again.

Meanwhile, Ann was once again sitting on the stone wall taking in all that surrounded her. Soon Jenny joined her. "Annie, you are going to miss these fields, aren't you?"

"Oh, yes, Jen. I don't want to go. I love it here: my climbing trees and the river I race on my way to work. Oh, the sound of the Tweed this time of year! Listen, Jenny." They both sat in silence listening to the roar of the Tweed, a sound they both had heard from the time they were wee babes. "Oh, Jenny, let's stay. I can stay with you," Ann begged.

"I would love to stay here with you, but how would we live? There is no more farm for us, Annie, and I could not work enough to support us both."

"But you could marry Fergus. Yes!" Ann began excitedly, "you could marry Fergus, stay here, and I could work longer for Baron Bryden, and we would be fine."

"Annie, what about Ma and Da and the boys? You would never see them again."

"Yes, I would. I would sail to America for a visit when I am old enough." She jumped down from the wall and began pacing as she did whenever she was excited. "I will miss them, but I will miss this more," she opened her arms and twirled around. "Please stay with me, Jenny, please."

"I can't, Annie. I just can't, and if I do stay, Ma and Da will not let you stay here."

"Why not?"

"For God's sake, Annie, because they love you and because your brothers love you."

"Well, I love them too, but I still don't want to leave."

Jenny looked out over the river; her thoughts were bleak. She had no more choice than Annie did. Even if she stayed here, she could never be with John, and though she was fond of Fergus Walton, it was difficult to think about being in his arms like she was with John. If she went to America, she would be leaving her love behind, but if she stayed, she would no longer have a place to live. If her grandparents took her in, she would still never see John, since she would have no reason to come here.

Ann looked over at Jenny. She knew who was filling her thoughts, and she knew her talk of staying here was all talk. Ann knew she had to go with her family. There was no choice for her. Jenny had the choice to stay or go. "Are you going to see him tonight?"

"I want to. I need to see him one more time. Da said that I have to help with packing and loading all day tomorrow. Annie, who am I kidding? I know I will go to America with my family because that is where I belong."

"I know. Me too. Go see him, Jen. I'll tell Ma you forgot to do something over at Mr. Scott's and that you will be late."

"Good. Thank you, Annie; you are such a good sister. I love you." She hugged Ann who quickly wiggled out of her embrace.

"Ok then, off you go. Hurry. You should be hugging him, not me."

She watched Jenny run toward the tall tower, turned, and ran smack into her brother, Tom.

"Where's she going?"

"Uh, I don't know, Tom. I think she needed to run down the path one more time and so do I." Annie turned and sped off like a lion. Tom knew where Jenny was going and it puzzled him that she would hesitate about going with the family to America. He was a serious boy who wanted to be just like his father. He loved farming and was excited about sailing to a new land. He went out to the barn one more time. Soon, this would no longer be his home. He loved the smell of the sweet straw and the pungent horse scent that emanated from the barn. How many times had he fallen asleep in this pile of straw? Tom knew one thing for sure: first thing in America, he would get himself a horse. He loved Ginger, the horse he had raised from a foal. Of course, they could not take her or any of the animals. They did not own them. All this land and everything on it belonged to Lord Buccleuch. The two dogs did not, but they could not afford to take them on the ship, so Wright Bryden had taken one, and Mr. Harrison had taken the other. He ruffled the long hair on Eildon's neck. He had named him after the three hills he saw every morning. Eildon was a sheep dog and a good one. Tom kneeled, put his face in Eildon's fur, and cried. "You will be a good boy for Mr. Harrison. Joseph will love you and take care of you." Joseph was Mr. Harrison's ten-year-old son.

Tom was a loner. He was taller than his father with the same eyes, but he had inherited the large English nose, that his face had not grown into yet, so when his hair was wet and slicked back he looked like a rat. To top it all off, he was as skinny as a starving dog, and the kids teased him saying he was so thin he could hide behind a snowflake. Hence, he surrounded himself with his animals. He talked to the sheep, Ginger, and Eildon, and he was rarely seen without his dog. The only human friend he had was his father and a boy from school who had moved to Canada three years ago. Since that time there had been no friends, boy or girl. "Maybe in America I will meet someone," he thought as he turned and looked down the path that Jenny had taken, wondering why she wasn't back yet.

Jenny would not be back for some time. Just as she passed the cottage house, the teacher, James Dodds, a distant cousin, came out with a pipe in his hand and sat in the rocker on the front porch. "Hello Jenny."

"Oh, you startled me," Jenny said; "how are you this evening?"

"Oh, fine, just fine, and what are you doing here at this hour?"

"Whatever do you mean? It is only five o'clock?"

"Well, you normally come in the morning. Isn't that right, Lass?"

"Uh, yes, but I can't come tomorrow, so I am here to say goodbye to Mr. Scott, cook, and Charles."

"Oh, yes, I heard you were setting sail soon. How brave of your father."

"I don't see what brave has to do with it. It is getting too hard to make a living here, and according to our letters from America, making a living for regular people is easier."

"Yes, if you have enough money or if you are willing to work as a servant for many years."

James took a long drag on his pipe. Jenny saw the smug, pompous look on his face. He was related, but thank God it was distant. "So, James, I heard you are going, too. I heard you got fired but Mr. Scott is letting you stay on until the end of the month."

"Well, that is simply not true," he huffed; "I am not fired. I am choosing to leave and go to law school."

"Uh huh," Jenny muttered knowing he had just told her a lie. "Okay, if that is what you are going with, that is fine. Good Luck. Maybe we will meet in America."

"We won't. You won't see me in that savage place fighting Indians and freezing to death in the snow. You do know how dangerous this little endeavor of father's is, don't you?"

"I am sure he knows the danger and will not put us at risk."

"Right. Well, let me enlighten you a bit, Lassie. Sailing across that sea to Newfoundland is putting you at risk. For example, there is the prospect of pirates robbing you, and if you even make it past those buccaneers, the treacherous sea waters of the Atlantic can capsize a ship. Then there is the British Navy conscripting men and boys off these ships. I haven't even mentioned diseases and starvation should you run into a delay and…."

"Excuse me, Sir, but I think you have mentioned plenty, and I am not intimidated in the least. Now, I bid you good night as I have come to see the Scotts, not you." Jenny abruptly turned and walked away. She knew there was some ancient history between these families, and now she knew it was still alive and well in James. Her father had never discussed the reason, but she always knew the distance was there. Jenny climbed the steps to the magnificent stone house, pulled the iron knocker on the door, and tapped it twice. Soon Charles opened the door. No matter what time Jenny came to the house, Charles donned the same outfit, black pants, white shirt, black bow tie, and a long black suit coat. He was very stiff and formal, but his small brown eyes always had a hint of kindness in them.

"Miss Jenny, how nice to see you. The master is dining. Should I set another place?"

"No, Charles. Thank you. I just came to say goodbye." She made her way down the hall toward the large dining area. There sat John and his uncle at the large rustic pine dining table.

"Ah, Jenny, do come in," Uncle Walter said, as she came through the arched dining doorway. "We are just finishing up, but Charles could get you a plate."

"No, thank you. He already asked."

"To what do we owe this visit? Have you come to say goodbye?"

"Yes, I am afraid so," Jenny whispered willing the tears to hold back.

"Well, I am off to my study. Jenny, you have been a wonderful employee and friend to John. You did get my recommendation letter I left with your mother, didn't you?"

"Yes, yes Sir, and thank you. It was very nice."

"Okay, I take my leave." He hugged her and then retired to his study. Jenny sat down at the table next to John. She had never told him about the possibility of marrying Fergus but she had told him about maybe moving in with her grandparents. Either way, he knew she would be leaving.

"Jenny, I can't believe you are leaving. I am going to miss you so much."

"Me too. I had to come tonight, since tomorrow I have to help my family with the packing and won't be able to see you. John, I am going to America with my family."

"I thought you would and you should. Even if you stayed with your grandparents, we would not be able to see each other."

"I know," Jenny whispered as tears welled up in her eyes.

"Come with me," John said as he took her hand. They walked out the door and toward the stables. As soon as they entered the barn, they were in each other's arms, and the passion engulfed them with the power of a freight train. They fell into the hay pile and made love one last time vowing to never forget one another. It was dusk before Jenny forced herself to go. They kissed one more time and walked hand and hand to the entrance of the path. Jenny was sobbing openly, tears streaming down her face. John watched as she turned one last time, smiled, and faded into the night. On the other edge of night, another man watched: James Dodds.

CHAPTER XI

The night before their departure, Jenny told Fergus that she was leaving. "Fine, Jenny, I will get my ticket in the morning. There are always openings on these British freight vessels."

"British. We are going on a British ship?"

"Yes. Those navigation laws they put on North American ships are still in effect, so there are only British ships going from here to Newfoundland. Under these acts, British colonies can import and export goods only in English vessels, and three-fourths of each crew has to be English."

"But what does that have to do with us?"

"Most of the ships carry cargo and passengers," Fergus explained. This was all good to know, but the matter at hand was Fergus and her decision.

"Did I hear you right, Fergus, you are going?"

"Of course, I am going because you are marrying me, aren't you?"

"What?" She took a deep breath and began, "I am so sorry, Fergus, but I cannot agree to marry you. I know you love me, but I do not feel the same. I am so sorry."

"I understand, Jenny, but I just do not want to let you get on that ship unprotected."

"Unprotected? My da will be with me. He has protected me all my life. I will not need protection from you."

"Okay, okay, Jenny, but just be alert. The crews on these ships are rough characters, and some of the passengers may be criminals released from British jails being shipped to the colonies."

"Fergus! That cannot be true. You're just saying that to scare me into staying."

"No, I'm not. It is true, Lass."

Jenny looked at him, surprised that he would do this to her. This was a manipulative side of Fergus she had never seen before. "Well, nevertheless, I assure you, I will stay away from those terrible criminals," she answered sarcastically. "Now, you must go, Fergus." She ushered him to the door, hugged him, and said goodbye. She watched him from the window as he walked slowly to his horse, looked one last time at the house, waved, and slowly trotted on down the glen. Now Jenny was glad she had made the decision to reject Fergus. She did not tell her parents that he had offered to leave Scotland. When she went to bed that night, she dreamed of tall green pines, blue waters, and mountains that stretched to the clouds.

Their debts paid and with a little cash in hand, Thomas and Helen Dodds and the six children set out on their journey early the next morning, April 30, 1819. The first thirty-five miles were the hardest. The road from Lessudden to Edinburgh was a mere track and the horse-drawn cart carrying their goods groaned and tipped under the weight of the load. They skirted Gala Water, a tributary of the River Tweed, through dirt and mire. The smaller children and Helen rode in the cart while Jenny, Thomas, Robert, and Ann walked most of the way. Because it was still spring, the road became muddy at times, and they had to help the driver push the vehicle through several mud puddles. It was seven o'clock when the driver announced that they could go no further this night. He pulled the cart into a wayside inn. The company had told Thomas that the drivers traveled all night, switching drivers along the way. With this unplanned stay, Thomas decided to have the children sleep in the cart; he and Tom would sleep on the ground. The weather was cool but not cold, and they had blankets.

"Nay," said the driver, "I'm locking this up in the livery. Can't sleep in it."

"I don't understand," Thomas said. "These are our possessions. Do you think we'll steal our own things?"

"Nay, not your things, the company things like the horse and cart. Sorry, but you'll have to sleep in the inn tonight." Thomas was too tired to argue. They went into the inn where they were greeted with loud music, raucous laughter, and scantily dressed women. The highway inns were famous for being disgusting dives rampant with thieves, ladies of the night, and terrible conditions. That night Thomas and the boys slept on the filthy floor while the rest of the family slept in the bed. At first, Ann sat down on the bed expecting to sink into feathers. Instead, it felt like she was sitting on the stone wall that ran along the Tweed. When she laid down, she discovered that it also sloped from head to foot. Helen took one look at the sheets and instructed the children to sleep on top of them. She wondered if it would not have been better for all of them to sleep outside, but at least in here they could shut and lock the door. She would not want her family vulnerable to the likes of those she had seen downstairs.

After itching and tossing and turning most of the night, they arose early the next morning. Thomas went to the driver's door and banged on it until he woke him. They were on their way by morning's light and reached Edinburg around noon where comfortable lodging was available. There was a good road for the remaining forty miles to Glasgow, and a regular stagecoach, the Fly, which made the trip on a five-hour schedule. The children were excited when they saw the coach and the carrier (driver). The driver sported a smart red coat, with black trousers and black boots. George, kept pointing and saying, "Soldier, soldier."

"No, George, he isn't a soldier," Tom, Jr. told him as he lifted him high above his head, so George could see better.

"Soldier," George repeated as he pointed to the man. Meanwhile the carrier of the cart holding their goods began unloading.

"Hey, mates, let's get this thing unloaded. I got more trips to make." With that, the children except for George and Mary began helping to unload the cart they came on, and the 'soldier' began loading it onto the sides and top of the stagecoach. Four horses pulled The Fly. Six passengers filled the inside, and the seats on top held four people. Of course, Ann rode on top along with Thomas and Tom. The horn blowing, whip cracking, and harness jingling delighted little

Mary and George as the driver whisked them away to Glasgow where they stayed at another, much cleaner, inn. However, even with the jingle of the coach bells and the children's laughter, fear of an uncertain future never left the thoughts of Thomas and Helen Dodds.

From Glasgow, there were still twenty miles to go. The town of Greenock commanded the great bulk of shipping, so that is where they would leave Scotland. This road was smoother, so the last lap of the overland journey went well, but with each mile all Jenny could think about other than her queasy stomach was how much farther away she was from John.

While in Greenock, Thomas bought a large quantity of Dominican mahogany lumber. Many ships, American and British, traded between Greenock and the West Indies. The hazards encountered by these ships differed from those in the North Atlantic. Instead of northern gales and ice, they had to look out for hurricanes and pirates when they were in the blue southern water. The great buccaneers who captured cities and whole countries had mostly disappeared from the Spanish waters; however, they were replaced by as mean a race of maritime thieves as the buccaneers had been. Nevertheless, the profits on outbound merchandise from the British Isles and inbound rum, molasses, and sugar were worth the risks. Now the modern furniture style popularized by Wollaston, Chippendale, Sherraton, and Hepplewhite, all British carpenters, enabled these ships to profit from space the crew would have filled with sand and bricks to keep the ship upright. These British vessels were narrow, deep, flat sided, and full-bottomed, which made bad vessels in the sea—slow and volatile in that they rolled heavily—and often needed ballast even when loaded to keep them from capsizing. Therefore, the ship's captains were delighted to take on heavy freight. Thomas had heard that the Americans needed furniture and that the fee for shipping was cheap because of this need for weight; he bought 10,000 board feet of mahogany weighing two and a quarter ton before sailing.

"You what?" Helen said. "But I thought you were only going to buy enough to make our own furniture. How could you, Thomas? How much money do we have left?"

"Enough, Helen, do not worry. We have enough." Thomas knew they barely had enough to get to Canada, much less America. The wood was such a good deal, he could not pass it up, and he knew if he had his tools he could sell his furniture to the Americans. Wright Rule had written about how important his carpenter's skills would be in America. The only problem was that Thomas loved wood like a gambler loves cards, and his favorite was mahogany, so he may have gone a little overboard. He should have taken Helen instead of Tom with him when he went shopping. Thomas sighed; 'oh well,' he thought; 'it is done.' He was glad they had packed more than enough smoked herring for the trip. They might be living on it for some time.

While Thomas inspected the wood inventory slips, the rest of the family wandered the moor until they saw an immense ship with the name, *The Protector*, printed on its side.

"That's it," Tom said. "*The Protector*, the name of our ship."

"Well that is a good name," Ann shouted above the sounds of the rigging chains and shouts of the men on the docks, "but it is so big."

"I know," Jenny replied. She looked up at the top of the mast and saw a figure moving up the pole. "Oh my gosh. Look at that man up there!" They all looked up. After a moment, Helen realized that it was too small to be a man.

"Where is Robert?" she asked everyone. They all looked around shouting his name.

"It's him. It's him!" shouted Mary. "I can see his scarf, the one I made for him for Christmas. It had yellow in it. It's him, Ma. Robert is almost at the top."

"That dolt!" Tom shouted. "Not only could he fall, but we could lose our passage."

Helen ran over to where Thomas was looking over the wood. "Thomas, we need help! Hurry!" He looked up, saw Helen's face, and began to run with her.

"What? What is it?" he asked, almost out of breath.

"Look!" Helen pointed to the huge ship.

"What? The ship. Yes, I saw it."

"No, Da," Mary cried; "it's Robert. Look where he is." They were all pointing at the main mast of the ship holding the sails. Thomas looked up and sure enough, perched high up on the pole and still climbing was Robert.

"What? That is Robert? Are you sure?"

"Yes, we are."

"How? How did he even get on the ship?"

"They just put the plank up for the crew to start loading. He must have sneaked on between the freight loads. Oh, my God, Thomas, do something. How is he going to get down?"

Thomas stared at the miniature figure on the mast. This was not good. The captains on these ships did not need a reason to refuse passage to anyone, and this would be a good reason. Many captains would see this as a hazard, an undisciplined child allowed to run around on the ship. All Thomas could do was speak with the captain and hope for the best. He tried to board the ship, but the crew abruptly stopped him. "But, I have to speak to the captain."

"No, you cannot board yet, and the captain is busy. You must wait your turn like everyone else," the sailor explained.

"But look," Thomas pointed. The man looked up and saw the boy halfway up the pole.

"That is your boy?"

"Yes, now please get the captain for me before he falls."

"The captain will not talk to you. I will get the first mate."

"Can't you just go up and get my boy down?" Helen pleaded.

"That is not our job." The first mate was a burly man with red curly hair. He said, "He has to come down sometime, so he will, but I am sure you will be hearing from the captain." He turned and walked away. Soon a man dressed in a blue coat and round white captain's hat appeared on the ship rail. Thomas saw him speaking with the red-headed man and watched him look up toward young Robert. He began his descent down the plank and stood in front of Thomas.

"I am the skipper of this ship, and I see your boy has run away from you."

"Yes, please have someone get him down."

"No, but you may enter, get him down, and then leave."

"What? We can't leave. We are sailing to Newfoundland on this ship."

"No, you are not. We cannot risk the ship's and our passengers' safety. Your undisciplined child could endanger everyone."

"But he is just a boy," Helen interjected. "He likes to climb."

"I see that, and there many other things he could climb on this ship. You will not sail on this ship." The skipper turned and began walking back up the plank.

"But you have already loaded half of my mahogany boards!" Thomas shouted as he saw the men carrying the boards below.

The skipper stopped, turned around, and shouted back, "What is your name?"

"Dodds, Thomas Dodds."

"You are the Thomas Dodds who bought all the mahogany boards?"

"Yes, yes I am," Thomas replied. By now, the whole family was standing with Thomas. Helen was wringing her hands. She had heard everything. "My Lord, where would we go? What would we do?" They had no home in Scotland anymore, and little did she know, but they did not have enough money to get back there anyway.

Fortunately, for the Doddses, this freighter did not have heavy cargo and therefore would have to buy sand and bricks to keep the ship upright. The captain was delighted to load the extra weight of the mahogany. As suddenly as the skipper told Thomas he could not sail, he shouted to him to come aboard, get his boy. Thomas walked up the plank, reached the skipper, and apologized for his son. In the meantime, Robert had climbed down onto the deck.

"Da, did you see me? Did you see me? I climbed the pole all the way to the top."

The skipper looked down at the boy, "And you will not do that again or climb anything again on the ship? Do you understand?"

Robert was surprised that what he had done was such a terrible offense. He knew he could climb like a monkey and could not see any danger of falling, but he did understand the sternness in this officer's voice. "Uh, yes, yes Sir," Robert said as he saluted him.

"You know what we do with men who don't follow orders?"

"Uh, no."

"No...."

"Uh, no Sir."

"We make them walk the plank." Robert's mouth dropped open and his eyes widened as he heard this terrible consequence.

"So, you climb nothing on my ship unless I say so."

"Yes, Sir."

"Now, get off my ship until we are ready to board." Robert shot off the ship like a rocket.

The skipper turned to Thomas. "Dodds, you keep an eye on that boy or I will snatch him for my crew. He climbed that pole better than most of my men." He smiled, nodded his head, and walked away.

"Thank you, Sir. I will keep an eye on him," Thomas replied, his heart beating so fast that he had to sit on the ground after getting off the ship. In the meantime, Helen was on Robert paddling his behind with her wooden baking spoon. He was young enough to discipline, but another year and the spoon would no longer work. Thomas was grateful for his wife who knew he was just too exhausted to handle anything else right then.

On May 2, 1819, at 7:00 AM, they boarded the ship, *The Protector*, to begin their journey to an unknown land. They unpacked their personals below and came back up to the rails to watch the outgoing tide carry them down the Firth of Clyde. With heavy hearts, they watched Ben Nevis hill and the hills of Renfrew slowly fade from sight until all that remained were the gray icy waters of the northern Atlantic Ocean.

Gail Huntley

CHAPTER XII

Being at sea was difficult for both crew and passengers. The skippers, mates, and jackies belonged to the lowest stratum of British social order, which, according the chronicles of those days, was low. They were coarse, vulgar, ignorant men who smelled like cheap rum and stale tobacco. They had a jargon of their own, and most could barely speak or write in their own language. The captains were good sailors, but much of the time, they had only a general idea of where they were.

The captain navigated by compass, intuition, and calculation of the speed of the ship by using a log. He gave the sailor at the helm a compass course to steer by and then calculated the speed with a log line knotted about every 50 feet. A crewman spun the log off a reel over the stern and timed the speed of it with a sand glass. The rate at which the knots ran out gave the speed. The captain figured the number of miles the ship traveled by the speed and the course given. Their exact position at any given time was more an intuitive guess by the captain than a calculated pinpoint location. Therefore, the adventure of sailing to a new land was a risky enterprise, even aside from the incumbent health risks.

The first to get seasick was Jenny, so all she remembered of the first few days was eating nothing and heaving over the side of the boat. Because the ship was so bottom heavy, it swayed on the waves like a weighted balloon toy that when punched returns to the same position. The government at that time taxed the ships on weight, so the top sails were made as light as possible. Soon, with the endless listing, Helen was also sick, which resulted in fewer adults to watch what Robert and Mary were doing. These two found plenty to be up to on the ship. The very first secret place they found was the captain's room. They sneaked in behind the cabin boy when he entered to swab the floors. Robert was thrilled with the maps, the telescope, and all the tools on the large desk. However, the second time they went in, the captain caught them and scuttled them out with a harsh scolding. Then they discovered they could hide under the lifeboats from Da or Ma who always wanted them to do something.

One week after setting sail, the captain announced that there was rough water ahead. "Nothing to worry about, folks. This old schooner can get through anything." To the average person watching this great machine maneuver through the choppy waters, it looked like a flying angel with its many wings spread out. *The Protector* was a beautiful sight with its white sails blooming out like curtains in the wind, but the captain and the crew knew the risks this vessel could run into in a storm.

Looking out at the horizon, Tom was the first to see the dark, ominous clouds rolling in like black tumbleweeds. They stretched for miles across the sky turning everything dark and damp. 'This is not good,' he thought, 'not good at all.' Minutes later, the captain ordered all women and children below deck. He also added, "There is nothing to worry about; it is just a spring storm, so we'll have some rough waters for a stretch." The captain ordered all men on deck in case he needed extra hands.

Thomas looked down the rail and saw Helen, Jenny, and Ann running up and down the deck shouting, but with the blasting sheets of rain plummeting the deck and the angry waves banging against the bow, no one could hear them. He ran down to his wife, "Helen, get the children down to the berth before it gets too rocky!" he shouted above the sound of the thundering waves hitting the boat.

"I know; I'm trying, but I can't find Mary!" she shouted back.

"Take the rest of them down. Tom and I will look for Mary." Thomas had sailed a few times on fishing schooners and had experienced some high winds and waves, but he had never experienced a large storm at sea.

By the time Helen and the children, including a fighting mad Robert who thought he was old enough to stay on deck, arrived down below, the boat was rocking like an empty bottle bobbing on top of the waves. Ann no sooner had her feet on the floor when the ship listed heavily to the right causing her to slide across the aisle smashing her back up against the ladder. This action blocked Mary's descent (Thomas had found her and put her on the top rung of the ladder). Because Ann hit the ladder, Mary missed the second step and fell on Ann.

"Ow!" screamed Ann. "Mary, get off me!" Mary had grabbed onto Ann's shoulders and was holding on as her feet dangled loosely several feet from the ship floor. 'Oh my God,' thought Ann, 'this is like the silo with Robert.' As the ship righted itself, Ann's quick thinking kicked in, "Okay, Mary, hold onto me, and we'll go down." Mary held on while Ann reached up, grabbed the ladder, and began stepping down with Mary holding on. Soon Mary's feet touched the floor.

"I'm down, Annie. Thank you."

All of them made it down the ladder, even with the ship lurching precariously back and forth with the will of wind. Suddenly, Robert began protesting again about being sent down with the women and children; he began climbing back up the ladder. Thomas saw him, wrapped his fist around his son's collar, and lowered him back through the hole. "But, I want to stay up there with you and Tom. I'm not a baby," Robert whined.

"No, you stay down there, Robert, and take care of your sisters and your ma." Thomas shouted as he let go of Robert's collar. Thomas rarely put a hand on his children, but he did not back away should the deed need to be done. He had no time to deal with Robert's complaints now, and he knew they could not have him above deck, underfoot, or climbing something on this swaying ship.

"Aye, aye, Sir," Robert replied. He felt better knowing that he had a task to do, a man's task. He turned and slipped on the last wrung of the ladder and fell face first into a barrel of flour cook had placed there before hauling it into the kitchen. When Robert righted himself, he heard laughter. He stood up, turned around, and stared straight into young Sabra Kellogg's pretty face. He was horrified that she and all the passengers were laughing at him. He felt the heat rise into his face like a hot August wind. Cook, a potbellied, wild, gray-haired man, came out just then with his fist raised, screaming at Robert.

"Get out of my flour, you rapscallion, or I'll skin ya alive!" he hollered as he raised his cleaver high over his head.

"I'm sorry. It was an accident," Robert cried, ducking down. "Here, I can put some of it back," and with that he started brushing the flour off his arms pushing it back into the barrel.

"Lordy, Lad. No! Where is this lad's folks?"

Helen spoke up, "I am here. Robert, get over here this minute!" Robert gladly moved away from the crazy cook and stood by his mother's side. Helen put her arm around his shoulders. "Mister, it was an accident. The ship rolled, and Robert fell; why is there a cask of flour out here in the first place?"

"Because I'm trying to clear the kitchen of critters, and don't want them jumping into the barrel."

"Critters?" Jenny asked. "What critters?"

"Just rats, miss. Just rats and a few snakes that make their way into my kitchen. Nothing to bother about. I got it all under control. Now, you need to keep your wee ones under control." They all sat momentarily stunned unable to speak except to whisper, "Rats."

"Wonder what he is doing with the rats?" Sabra Kellogg piped up.

"What kind of meat you think is in our supper, Sabra?" Robert asked, as he grinned, wiped the flour from his face, and sat down.

"What?"

"Oh Sabra, he is teasing you," Helen soothed as she glared at Robert and shook her head.

"Yup, Sabra, I'm joking. I saw him burning those rats in the stove. Besides, the only meat we've had since we started last week is fish."

"That's right," Sabra replied.

"Unless it wasn't fish," Robert added.

"Robert Dodds, stop it right now," Helen scolded. "Sabra, do not listen to him. We are not eating rat meat. She turned to Sabra's mother. So sorry, Ruby, my son thinks he is a jokester."

"It's okay, Ruby assured her, it's kind of nice to have some humor now and again on this ugly old ship" Through all the turmoil from the storm and Robert, Helen had not noticed that Jenny was missing. She looked around, but Jenny was no longer in the hold. She excused herself from Ruby, rose up and hanging on to anything she could, made her way to the bathroom. She found Jenny vomiting in the latrine, again sick from the ship bouncing on the angry waves. Helen rubbed her back and helped Jenny to the cot where she promptly fell asleep beside George who was also sick.

Meanwhile, on the top deck, the crew was busy. One man had climbed the pole and lowered the sails while others tied down chairs and other items that were sliding back and forth across the deck. A crew member hollered for Thomas and Tom to come help him. The lifeboat was swinging out over the open water. One of the ties had come loose, and the mate could not pull it back by himself. Thomas and Tom ran over, grabbed the large rope, and began pulling. However, not having the right boots, they kept sliding on the slippery deck. When the lifeboat was within a foot of the ship, Tom took a breath, sighing with relief. But relief was not to be because at that very moment hell came calling with a monster wave jutting up like a giant rising far above them. Tom yelled, "Wave!" just as the wave bore down on them, washing the screaming crew member out to sea. Tom felt himself sliding toward the edge of the boat. The rope was now dangling; if he continued to hold it, it would take him out over the black waters. He could not see anything except a dull light making its way through the wall of water. He looked for his da. When he did not see him, his heart sank; he knew that his father was gone. He had been on the same side as the crewman who had gone over. Just as Tom was about to go over the edge himself, he felt someone grab his arm and pull him in. A stinging pain jabbed him in his side as he smashed against a hard, round object. "Here, Mate, hold on! Hold onto the rail!"

The skipper put Tom's hands on the rail. His fingers automatically grabbed and curled around the shiny wet bar. He hung on with both hands as the rail dipped dangerously close to the ceiling of the ocean. Tom looked around for his da and saw nothing but the spray of salt water slapping and stinging his face. As fast as the wave came in, it went. The mammoth wave rolled on toward land leaving the rising sun rays glinting across the rolling water. Tom turned and saw a large, pale-faced man. He stood a head and a half taller than

Tom, who was nearly six feet. Tom remembered seeing him on the loading dock. He remembered him because the man limped and had a long yellow braid that hung down the middle of his back.

"You okay, Mate?" the man asked.

"Oh, yes, yes. I guess so. Are you the one who helped me?"

"You mean kept you from being shark food?"

"Yes."

"Well than, aye, Mate, it was me."

"Thank you, Sir. Thank you so much. Have you seen my father?"

"I don't know what your father looks like. All I saw was you."

"Please, we have to find him!" Tom shouted, panic exploding inside him.

"Hey, you. Stop your jabbering and get over here!" shouted one of the officers. The man with the braid turned at once and raced over to the officer. Tom began frantically looking for Thomas. He went back to the rail where only minutes ago they were both standing. After ten minutes of searching, he had to assume that the ocean had taken his father. He headed for the officer's quarters to report him missing when he saw the yellow-haired man coming back with the officer and another man. As they came into view, Tom realized the other man was his father.

"Da!" He shouted, breaking into a run.

"Tom!" The two men met and embraced.

"Da, I thought you went over the rail."

"And I thought the same about you. The last I saw of you, you were dangling from the rope. I tried to get to you, but that wave washed me clear over to the other side of the ship. When I stood up, you were gone."

"This man saved my life," Tom told his father. "Wait!"

"What is your name?" Tom asked.

"Danny. I'm Danny Kellogg."

"Kellogg. You got a relative on board?" Thomas asked.

"Oh, William and Ruby?"

"Yes, I think that was their names. We met them the first day."

"I saw their names on the manifest. I think he is my grandfather's brother from Ireland, but I am not sure since I have never met them. I plan to before the end of the trip, though."

"Ireland, huh? Well, I'm Thomas Dodds and this is my son, Tom," He offered his hand. "Thanks for saving my son, Danny. We're from Scotland. Are you also from Ireland?"

"Oh no, from all over, I guess, but I was born in a village on the eastern border of Ireland. We moved to Huntly, Scotland, when I was a wee lad. Where are you going?"

"To America. A place called New York."

"I'm headed that way too. Just working to save a little money to buy some land up in the mountains of that state."

"What mountains?"

"Old mountains that come down from Canada into New York. Hardly any people live there now, but my cousin says the land is cheap, the waters are as clear as that blue sky, and the woods are peppered with game."

The ship's officer quickly whisked Danny away to tend to his duties. The ship's doctor/second mate checked out Tom's injured side and diagnosed a cracked rib, taped him up, and told him he would be fine in a few days. Tom and Thomas climbed down below to check on the family. Ann had a sore back for a few days, and Robert had an injured ego. Soon, even Jenny was getting some pink in her cheeks after what seemed like endless vomiting.

It was not long before the children discovered the chickens trapped under a lifeboat. Mary thought it exciting to have animals sailing with them and promptly named them all. Soon George and Mary were visiting them every day, sneaking under the lifeboat and playing with the chicks. They also played hide and seek, hiding under the lifeboats. One afternoon when Mary came out of her hiding place, she left the entrance door up letting several chickens and the rooster out. As soon as she saw what she did, Mary tried in vain to get them back under the boat. When she failed do that, she ran away and hid. Within the hour, she watched as the frantic crew tried to get the chickens back under the lifeboat. Many of the birds flew up on the rail and then plunged overboard to their deaths.

Later, Mary heard the passengers talking about how they might not survive now that their main source of food was almost gone. The largest staple had been the chickens and their eggs, and all but two of the chickens were gone. The rooster was gone, and the chickens would not lay eggs now. She heard people guessing who had done it, and how it could have happened; some even had a theory that a spy from a competing shipping company sabotaged the ship. "You did it, didn't you?" Robert queried Mary.

"I did not. I did not do it!" Mary snapped back. "Why accuse me? Maybe you did it!"

"Mary, I've seen you go under those boats."

Mary began to cry. "And now they are all gone. Drowned. I drowned them all, Robert. I should be drowned. Now we are going to go hungry. What have I done?" Robert put his arms around her and told her to hush. He pulled her over to a corner and explained to her that she must never admit this, as it would come down on Da.

"Mary, this will be our secret, Okay? We will never tell. Promise me."

"I promise," Mary uttered through her tears. She wiped them on her shirt and came out of hiding, never letting on that she knew anything about any chickens. She and her brother had a pact that they would keep forever.

Gail Huntley

CHAPTER XIII

JULY 1819

It would be nine long weeks before the great craggy rocks of the Newfoundland coast appeared on the horizon. Because the storm had blown the ship off course, it took longer than the normal six weeks for the voyage. As time passed, the passengers experienced the ramifications of the chicken losses. The captain rationed fresh water, giving most of it to the crew who needed it to stay alive to run the ship.

Helen seemed the strongest of the family, running around day and night tending to her own family and other families who had come down with scurvy due to the lack of fruit. This disease seemed to target the young and the elderly. One minute Tom was on deck learning about being a deck hand from his new friend, Danny, and the next minute he was flat on his back in his bunk unable to hear or see anything. His fever ran high, and just when Helen thought it could not get any worse, Ann began to experience the same symptoms. Helen and Jenny tended to them and prayed for the ship to reach shore before they all became sick.

Panic set in when the McDonalds, an elderly couple sailing to Nova Scotia to live with their children, died of tuberculosis. The crew wrapped their bodies in sailcloth, the captain read a passage from the Bible, and the passengers watched in horror as the couple was tossed overboard into the raging sea. Robert stood transfixed, tears streaming down his face because he had played cards with the McDonalds throughout the trip. They had been so excited to be seeing their children for the first time in years.

What started out as an exciting adventure to Robert was fast becoming a nightmare. The hull where the family stayed to avoid others with disease was dark, and at night the rats and mice scurried over and under them. During the storm, everything was closed up, making the stench of urine and sweat almost unbearable. While confined to quarters, the children longed to be on deck in the fresh sea air. Robert and Ann would sit on their bunks and talk about the clean air, the blue water in the locks back home, and the fresh apples hanging from the tree beside the barn.

After the captain lifted the deck ban, Robert was the first to race up the ladder and onto the deck, breathing in the fresh salt air that smelled sweeter than the scent of heather on the hills. However, his exuberance did not last long; he too had become fatigued from lack of nutrients. Just as several other passengers were close to death from one of the two diseases on board, a large ship appeared on the horizon. Robert saw it and thought it was a pirate ship. Dragging himself toward the stern of the ship looking for his father, he found him fixing a lifeboat that had cracked in the storm. "Da, a pirate ship is coming. Hurry!"

"What? There aren't any pirate ships anymore, Robert."

"Oh, that's not what I read. There are still some on this ocean, and there is one out there right now." Thomas followed Robert to the bow. "Over there; see?" Robert pointed.

Thomas looked over the rail and saw a ship bigger than the one they were on moving swiftly toward them, sails reaching toward the clouds. He saw a flag, but it was too far away to make out the emblem on it. By this time, Jenny, Ann, and Helen had come up on deck to get some fresh air. "What is it?" Helen asked.

"We are not sure, but Robert thinks its buccaneers."

"Pirates?"

"That's right," Robert said excitedly.

"For Lord's sake, Robert, if they are pirates, it is nothing to be happy about. They steal stuff and hurt people. It could be a British ship looking for men to conscript into their navy, though." Jenny added.

"They would do that?" Helen asked. She could not believe the Britons were doing that.

"They talk about that in pubs, Helen, but I don't think it is true," added Thomas, knowing full well it was true.

"Let's find Danny and see if he knows," suggested Tom. Tom knew Danny would know what kind of ship was approaching at full speed. They all began looking for him and found him on the port side preparing to lower the lifeboats. "What is going on, Danny?"

"Oh, we have a Canadian rescue ship bringing us food and a real doctor. We are sending our lifeboats over and I am rowing one of them. We cannot land in Newfoundland until the doctor gives us clearance."

"Clearance? What do you mean? After all this time we can't land?" Ann asked in exasperation.

"Land," Jenny added, "how far are we from land?"

Danny pointed toward the bow. "Look."

Barely visible through the unending mist Jenny could make out a shadow. "That. That is land."

"Yes ma'am. That is Newfoundland."

"Oh, my Lord! Land! Wait, did you say we can't go ashore?"

"No, ma'am, not until the doctor releases us from quarantine." The family watched as the lifeboats made several trips out to the ship. The first ship returned with a white-haired, white-bearded man carrying a black bag. He was the doctor who lived on the banks of Newfoundland in a small farming community. He was also the designated maritime doctor who saw to it that no ship with contagious diseases aboard entered Newfoundland. It would be another week before the Doddses could set foot on the shores of this rocky island. They jumped for joy when their feet touched the ground. Ann ran in circles twirling little George around as he squealed in delight. It was only later that she realized there were no trees on this gray, bleak land. Now she knew she would hate America. Now she knew she would not stay in this horrible place. When she grew up, she would be on a ship back to her beloved Scotland and trees; no one could stop her. But right now, she was happy to just to be on land, any land, stark or not.

Danny told them about a small inn on the peninsula where Thomas paid for a room that they all shared. Early the next morning, Helen woke everyone up. They ate porridge and walked down to the moored ship that would take them further into Canada on a large river called the St. Lawrence. Danny transferred onto this new ship, making his way to America too.

Watching the land disappear in the distance, Danny told them that the point they were rounding was called Cape Ray. Looking out on the horizon, they saw miles of choppy, gray water. The shoreline was no more inviting than the water. It was stark, rocky, and depressing. The mist-draped bluffs rose from the sea towering over them like citadels. Observing this landscape was both exhilarating and terrifying to the family. As the ship sailed toward the peninsula, Helen began to see a little green valley, spilling down to the water's edge. "Oh, look, Ann, there is green," but by the time Ann looked, the green ended in a second range of dark ominous mountains of rock. Ann and Helen were both thinking of the hills at home—purple heather blankets as far as the eye could see—as they passed by gray bluffs rising dramatically from the Gulf of St. Lawrence; masses of sheer rock towering off the rugged, windswept island. A feeling of foreboding swept through the family. They had survived a horrific storm, starvation, and several diseases on the trip across the Atlantic. Now they were approaching America, and the closer they came to this new land, the more uninviting it seemed. Where were the forests? Where were the green fields? Where was the fertile soil?

As they ascended the three hundred miles of lower river, the landscape improved. They passed villages, farms, and long narrow fields that streaked back from the water to the hilltops. The country grew more open. Suddenly, it closed in again. A lofty barrier lay, to all appearances, directly diagonal from the river. They learned it was the gigantic rock above Quebec, Canada. George was delighted with this giant monster looming ahead. Appearing before them were several towers and massive buildings that plunged into the clouds.

When the ship moored, and they were on solid ground, even Ann was appreciative of this unique town with the cathedral spires, narrow wooden buildings, and narrow streets. Upon seeing the tallest tower, Robert at once began plans to climb it. To his delight, the next day, unknown to his family, he wandered into the cathedral and met a priest who offered him a tour up to the bell tower. He went with the priest knowing Da would punish him if he found out he was in a Catholic Church and this far from the family. However, looking out over this city from so far above was thrilling to Robert. He thought, 'I would love to live here, high up in a tower.' Being up in the air was worth whatever punishment he would receive should Da find out.

The whole family was amazed at the size of the town, the many people scurrying up and down the streets, and the abundance of carriages offering rides for a fare. The only problem was that they could not understand anyone because these Canadians spoke in some outlandish tongue. In the lower town there were two good inns, the Exchange Coffee House and the Neptune, and many 'genteel boarding houses.' In the upper town there were others still more respectable, but out of their price range. Danny had told Thomas not to stay in the port as it was very expensive. He heeded his advice by staying on board the ship for a couple of days while he completed arrangements for continuing to Montreal. In the shipping building, there was a government official charged with the duty of giving information and aid to immigrants, and the official spoke some English. Thomas wanted to leave Quebec at once to save money and to avoid exposing his family to contact with people who spoke this strange tongue. Even more upsetting to Thomas and Helen were seeing the priests in shovel black hats and black soutanes and nuns in various habits seemingly on every corner of the street. This picture created a cold shudder within Thomas, a staunch Presbyterian from Lessudden, and so it was a good thing that he never learned of his son's jaunt into the Citadel with a man dressed in black, who took Thomas' name of 'Father.'

It was here that Tom said goodbye to his friend, Danny Kellogg. It was also here that Thomas told the family they were going to a place called Rossie in America after sailing to Montreal, Canada. Danny told Ann and Tom that the mountains he was going to were like the highland hills in Scotland but higher and with more trees. "My land borders a new settlement called Pendleton, and I will travel down a different path than you to get there. I will work for the British shipping company for a year and then move next spring in time for planting."

Ann's ears perked up when she heard one word, 'Trees.' "You said trees; what kind of trees?" Ann asked, thrilled to hear that this place had trees.

"Oh, all kinds, but mostly large green pines that reach up to the sky for many meters," Danny told her. She could not wait to tell Da about this Pendleton place in New York. However, when she told him, he told her that he thought they would be going west of there. Ann was so disappointed because she thought it may be all rock like what she had seen so far in Canada.

Two days later, Thomas bought third-class tickets for the women and children on a one hundred and eighty-foot sidewheeler river steamer called *The Hercules*, which was running between Quebec and Montreal. These cabin tickets were $2.50 including meals. Thomas, Tom, and Robert had deck passage, which was $1.00 for each. When Helen saw the steamer, she stood frozen in fear. This was not a ship. It was a boat, and it looked like a flimsy boat at that. It was much smaller than the one they had just left. "Thomas, we are not going on that thing, are we?"

"Yes, we are, dear. This is not the ocean. It is the St. Lawrence River."

Helen and Mary looked at the white caps cutting across this giant, fast-moving river. It looked scary to them. "Ma, I don't want to go on another boat. I want to stay here," cried Mary.

"Me too," sobbed George. "No more boat," and he began to cry.

Putting up a brave front, Helen assured the children that it was just a river and they would be on and off the boat before they knew it. However, when the steamer started up, the engines were so noisy that they could barely talk with each other, and they all felt the slam of the waves against the bow. Once again, Jenny was sick for most of the journey. Thirty-two hours later, Mary shouted for joy when the Montreal harbor came into view. Much to her chagrin, *The Hercules* had to wait to dock until another ship left. Robert wanted to swim in instead of waiting, and Jenny was ready to go with him. However, after another hour, the ship began to move, and finally they moored at Montreal harbor.

It was here that Thomas found out that steam navigation in the rapids section of the river was impractical, so they would need another mode of transportation to continue their journey. Thomas paid for a room at the Pomroy Inn, and after booking the room, they set out to explore the town. They had never been in a place with so many stores. Even Jedburgh, the large village Helen was from, did not have sidewalks, several clothing stores, fur stores, and stores that sold only hats. They entered a tailor's shop where a man was measuring another man for trousers.

"Ma, I need some new trousers," Robert said as he stuck his leg out showing the thin worn material covering his knee.

"Oh, my, yes, come with me young man," a man said in English.

They had not heard English in Quebec at all, and so far, everyone spoke French in Montreal, too. "Hello, you speak English," Helen remarked.

"Oh, yes, yes, though not too good."

"Oh no, it is good," Robert blurted out, delighted to hear English.

"Are you the owner of this wonderful store?" Helen asked.

"Oh yes. My grandfather, Pierre Desautels came here from France as an indentured servant around 1700. He bought land and farmed it even though he was a tailor trained by his father. So, I carry on the tradition. This is my son Celestin and my daughter Henriette. Now, what can we get you?" Helen told the man whose name she could not pronounce that they could not buy anything right then but that he had a lovely store; Tom Jr. stared so long at Henriette that Helen and Jenny had to almost push him out the door.

"Uh, oh, Tom is in love," teased Robert.

"No, I'm not," snapped Tom, but that night he dreamed of a tiny woman with coal black eyes and hair that shined like a raven's wing in the sun. The next day he returned to the store just before the ship left. She was alone. He told her about going to America. She been down the St. Lawrence and another waterway called Lake Champlain. Their time together was electric, and before he left, they knew this little moment in time, though their last, would be in their hearts forever. The last image he would see of Henriette Desautels was her beautiful face pressed against the window, watching him walk away.

Thomas saw his son coming toward the inn. "Where have you been?"

"Oh, I just wanted to get my land legs before we get on another ship."

"Well, we need to hustle and get loaded. Come on." With one last look at the little storefront shop, Tom turned and headed toward the stagecoach they would take on the next branch of their journey. It was nine o'clock in the morning when they began their twenty-six-mile coach journey to Lachine where they would hire a Durham boat from a Mr. Grant. Thomas arranged to send the mahogany by wagon.

Upon reaching Lachine, they boarded a thirty-five-foot boat. It had a sharp bow, a round stern, and a flat bottom. After boarding, Robert ran around and counted only five crew men. It was one hundred miles from Lachine to Prescott, and they would cover half the distance by boat, over Lake St. Louis and Lake St. Francis. Some stretches of the river were broad and placid enough to sail; however, the rest of the way, in the swift currents of the narrower reaches and in the rapids, the crew used heavy metal poles and long tow lines to move the boat ahead. There were many carries, and it proved to be a long arduous trip spent with men drinking kegs of raw whisky. When it rained, the crew handed out tarps; the passengers brought their own food and found their own lodging.

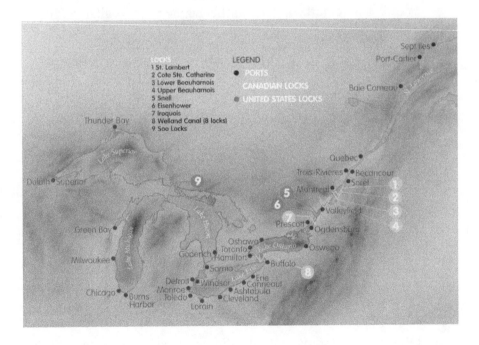

The Dodds spent several nights in farmhouses because they were cheaper than inns, and because Thomas did not want his children exposed to the goings on of the taverns. Several of the farmers who rented rooms were Loyalists who had escaped to Canada from the

United States. Consequently, these compatriots graciously received families from Scotland or England.

Jenny was no longer sick, but the trip had taken its toll on all of them. In addition, she became gloomier the further she was from John Scott. She could not stop thinking about him. At one of the farms, the owners came out and welcomed them. "Welcome to our home. I am John, and this my wife Mary Scott. Please come in."

Jenny heard nothing beyond John Scott. Without thinking, she blurted out, "I know a Scott, John Scott from Lessudden."

"Yes," Da remarked; "he is the nephew of Walter Scott, the writer."

At the mention of that name, John Scott replied, "Oh, yes, we have heard of them. They are distant relatives, but we do not know them. Our grandparents were from the highlands, though."

"So, you don't know John?" Jenny asked, trying to force an acknowledgment she knew was not there.

"No, Lass, we don't know him."

She turned and walked to her bed; she continued writing her letters to John, knowing she would never see him again and dreading the rest of the journey on the drunken sailor boat if they even made it to this horrible place. She hated this whole trip and sometimes secretly wished they would not make it. She did not want anything to happen to her family. She just wanted them to give up and go home.

But one way or another, by luck, manual strength, and hard liquor, the Durham boat was blown, shoved, and dragged all the way to Prescott. Robert, Mary, and George loved the boat, and if Thomas and Helen thought wistfully of the Brae Heads at Lessudden, or remembered looking down on the mighty Tweed, their homesickness was set aside by the necessity of keeping their children from falling overboard.

It would be early August when they reached Rossie. Ann was surprised that the land was cleared for pasture. Several friends in Scotland had told her the colonies were all forest. Instead, she looked out over green fields peppered with sheep. It reminded her of home except for the missing heather-laden hills.

In a place near Rossie called Ogdensburg, a German-born land speculator who moved to the United States in 1806 had built a stone hotel called, The American House. Several families of the first settlers were this man's guests until their cabins were ready. His name was David Parish, and he had bought 200,000 acres of land in the St. Lawrence valley and favored selling to Scottish immigrants because his grandfather hailed from Scotland. They stayed at this hotel for two days learning about the area before moving on to Rossie. It had been months since Helen had heard from her Uncle Wright, so she figured he was living somewhere else by now. When he lived in Scotland, he never stayed in one place for long.

The next day the family settled into a small cabin that previous settlers had left; but it was a temporary dwelling as relatives were coming in a month to live in it. David Parish had told Thomas about the cabin and apologized because it was so small. They were all amazed when they saw it. It was larger than their cottage in Scotland. Soon, they found the store that offered liberal credit to those who bought farms. Now that they had shelter and a plan, Thomas and Tom were excited about the farming prospects. Thomas found that his carpentry skills were in demand in this new developing land. Ann at once discovered the forest running along the edge of the pastures. She ran to the nearest tree, climbed to the top, and surveyed the brown fields, apple trees, and vegetable gardens stretching for miles. Looking out over the horizon, she saw the great river lined by large trees with five-fingered leaves and evergreens that shot up to the clouds like rockets. She knew looking out at this land that this was going to be better than she had imagined—she had trees, a river like the Tweed, and lush green fields. She dropped out of the giant maple tree and ran to the cabin, red pigtails flying in the wind.

Chapter XIV

It was not long after their arrival that Helen noticed Jenny was still pale and tired most of the time. Walking down the dirt road to the local store, Helen asked her if she was ill, Jenny said "No, I'm just tired from the trip."

"But that was days ago."

"I know. I guess maybe I have a touch of something and can't shake it." Helen thought that odd. When she entered the store with Jenny and little George, a large woman wearing a white bonnet, blue dress, and white apron rushed over. "Why, good morning to you, Helen."

Helen, looking confused, said, "Good morning; do I know you?" The woman began to laugh "Ah, 'tis a small settlement. We know already who is coming and who is going. Catherine here told me about you coming." Now Helen was even more confused. "Catherine?"

A tiny woman with chestnut brown hair peeking out from a gray bonnet stepped forward, "Hello. I am Catherine Rule, Helen, your aunt. Don't you recognize me?"

"Oh, my goodness; yes, I am so sorry, Aunt Catherine. I was so surprised that someone said my name; I did not even look your way. I am happy to see you again. How is Uncle Wright?"

"Oh, he is fine, just fine, out milking the cows. Well, welcome to our village." She hugged Helen and Jenny, then stepped away and said, "so is this your youngest?"

"Yes, this is George. George say hello to Aunt Catherine."

"Hello, Aunt Catherine. Ma, can I look around?"

"If you don't touch anything," Helen replied.

"He is delightful," Catherine remarked, smiling at him as he walked toward the candy. Catherine introduced them to the large woman. "Helen, this is Barbara Rule, your distant cousin."

"Oh my, Barbara, are you from Jedburgh too?"

"That I am, Lassie. Your father is my cousin. I knew you when you were a wee one, but we did not live close, so I did not see you as you got older."

Catherine interjected, "I know the cabin you are staying in. It's the old Dalzell cabin. They got their land last month. Well, that cabin will not do; that will not do at all. You will come stay with us until you have a place. How many children are there now?"

"Six."

"Six is fine. We have room. We can put the older boys in the barn loft. Helen, why didn't you write and tell us when you were coming? I wish you had come to us first."

"The last letter I received from you was almost a year ago, and I didn't know for sure where you lived."

"But I sent you a letter in December."

"I never got it."

"Darn mail. Well, that letter told you to come to us when you arrived, but, dear, you are here now, and you must stay with us until you get settled."

Helen's mind raced; this couple, though quite jolly, was also known to squabble, and Uncle Wright, well Uncle Wright…. "That is so kind of you, Aunt Catherine. Thomas and I will discuss it when he gets home." She looked around for George, but he had disappeared. "Now where did that child go? He was just here a minute ago."

"Oh, I saw my daughter, Teresa, take him out on the steps. They are playing marbles. I thought you saw. They can be a handful, and when is your bairn due, dear?" Aunt Catherine asked Jenny.

Jenny looked around thinking her aunt was addressing someone else. "What? Are you talking to me?"

"Uh, why yes, dear; when are you due?"

"But, Aunt Catherine, I am not pregnant."

Helen's mouth dropped open, and finally she sputtered out the words, "Catherine, Jenny is not having a baby."

"Oh no, I didn't realize…. I thought…. Oh my, I am so sorry."

"Am I getting fat, Ma?"

"Well, you have put on a bit but…."

"No, no, it is not that. She has the mask." They all looked and noticed the rash on one side of her face.

"Oh no, Catherine. Jenny had scurvy on the ship, and it left her with that rash even though she has mostly recovered."

"Oh, again, I apologize for jumping to conclusions." Just then, the bell rang, and the door opened.

They all turned toward the door and there filling up the doorway stood Fergus Walton.

"Fergus Walton! What? What are you doing here?" Jenny asked gasping for air.

"I have been here for two weeks."

Helen walked toward him, put her arms out, and hugged him. "Why, Fergus, what on earth?"

"After you left, I got to thinking and decided that this adventure sounded like a good one for someone such as myself." Jenny was speechless. She stood, frozen to the floor. She stared at Fergus, then shook her head and looked again, thinking she must be imagining this whole scenario: first her aunt's strange words about pregnancy and then Fergus' sudden appearance. Aunt Catherine's words shot at her like a canon rolling through her head as she remembered those two times with John Scott.

Lost in her fear, she was not aware that Fergus was moving toward her until he was directly in front and wrapping his arms around her. Like a zombie, she allowed him to hug her. However, his nearness did bring her into the present, and she returned his hug mumbling something about how they would have to get together and talk about their trips.

Fergus smiled, moved away, and addressed Catherine, "Well, Mrs. Rule, I need some supplies for Mr. Parish."

"Very well, Fergus. Now you folks think about coming and staying with us, and Sunday afternoon we will expect you for Sunday dinner. You too, young man."

"Yes ma'am, thank you; I wouldn't miss one of your dinners for anything."

"Hold on just a minute, Fergus, while I walk them out." Once outside, Jenny met her youngest cousin, fifteen-year old Stella. That night the family had a heated discussion about moving in with the horse thief and his wife. Helen heard very little; her mind was whizzing around like a steamboat paddle, reliving the trip, and thinking about how many times Jenny had been sick since they stepped off the boat.

That Sunday after church, they all gathered at the Rules for dinner. The Doddses accepted the generous offering of temporarily staying with the Rules. Wright Rule suggested that he and Thomas go hunting after dinner, and Jenny and Fergus went for a walk. Fergus explained that right after they left, he decided to go to the new land and bought passage aboard a ship leaving the next day. Since he did not have people or lumber and materials to ship, he was able to get there quickly. Nor did his ship hit any severe weather. He had arrived two weeks ago and had hired on with Mr. Parrish. Fergus would work for Mr. Parrish for two years, receive 100 acres on credit at $5.00 an acre, and pay it back in five years.

"It sounds like a lot of money."

"Yes, but it will be mine. Think of that. I will own 100 acres of land."

"Will you put sheep on it?"

"No, I will plant crops and raise cattle. That is more common over here. Jenny," he took her hands in his, "I would love to share this

151

with you if you would only have me. I know you do not love me as I love you, but you will. I promise, you will."

"I am sorry, Fergus, but the answer is still no. I can't think. We just arrived, and I am too tired to think about anything like that."

"Are you still sick, Jenny? I heard you and Helen were very sick."

"No, I don't think so, but I am still weak and tired from it."

"Very well. Then, let's return before I tire you out. I enjoyed our walk."

"As did I," Jenny replied. Later, that night, she wrote a letter to John Scott describing the beautiful rivers and green valleys of this new land.

That same night, just before dawn, Ann heard something outside of her window. She got up, looked out, and saw a large creature standing just outside the garden perimeter. She screamed and woke up the house; they all came running to her. She was so petrified that all she could do was point out the window and run to Thomas.

"What is it, Lass?" her father asked as he held her shaking body.

"Big. Black; shiny eyes; big, so big!" she gasped.

"Oh," Wright, said, "It's a bear."

"A what?" Thomas questioned.

"A bear," Wright replied, "we have bears here."

"What?" Helen asked her voice shaking. "But aren't they in the woods? Why are they near the house?"

"They come looking for food, but I am sure that one is all the way to Canada by now after Ann's screams," he chuckled.

"It's not funny, Uncle Wright. How come no one told us about these, these animals?" Jenny asked.

"No one asked," Wright replied. "We also have deer, moose, wolves, and other creatures that roam in the night." After that night, caution covered all of them. However, Thomas and Tom were delighted that now hunting would include bear, and it was not long before Thomas shot his first bear, Helen cooked her first bear meat, and Jenny got sick just smelling it.

If ever anyone was looking for Tom, he could find him out in the pasture with Wright's three horses. One evening after Wright returned from hunting, he walked over to Tom. "So, you like horses, I guess."

"Yes, I raised one from a colt in Scotland. I hated to leave him, and I miss him."

"Well, how would you like to have one of these?"

"What? Uncle Wright, but how?"

"Well, I ain't got a whole lot of time to tend them anymore, so if you take care of them, ride them, and make sure they're fed, after six months you can have this one." He put his hand on the back of a light brown horse. "This here is a Percheron mare, and you can ride and work her."

Tom was ecstatic. He couldn't believe his uncle would do this for him. Da still needed to buy more horses, but this would be his own horse. Then he remembered who he was talking to. He knew his father would not let him have a stolen horse. "Uh, Uncle Wright, where did you get this horse?"

"Where did I get it? Why I bought it over in Ogdensburg. Why?"

"Uh, well, there are stories...."

"Oh, yes, stories of my horse thieving days."

"Yes."

"Lad, these horses were not stolen. I was a wild young buck in my day, but your aunt has tamed me; only this one here is stolen." Wright walked over to a large gray workhorse and put his hand on him.

Tom's mouth dropped open, He thought, if one was stolen then probably this one was too. Now he was in a dilemma. He wanted this horse so badly, but he knew it was stolen. Maybe Da would never find out.

"Got ya worried some, huh? Can't decide what to do? You really want that horse, don't you?"

Tom shook his head. Just then Aunt Catherine came out and caught the tail end of the exchange between the two men.

"Tom, he's pulling your leg. We bought those horses. Wright, you are such a teaser." She walked over and put her arm around him. "You know, son, Wright was accused of stealing a horse, but they never proved it."

"A horse. I heard you stole several horses. Did you, Uncle Wright?"

"Yes I did, Lad, because the duke took my hunting dogs and sold them to somebody else."

"But weren't they the duke's dogs on his manor?"

"No, son they weren't; I bought them. They were my pets. I tried to explain it to him, but he sloughed me off like a pesky ant, so that night I got me a couple of pets from his border land. They knew it was me because your dad's cousin, James Dodds, turned me in for the reward the duke offered. Lord, don't let me ever see that relative again. Anyway, they never could find the horses, so though they accused me, they didn't arrested me right away, and I hightailed out of there before they could. Soon after I arrived here, I sent for your aunt and the kids, and been living this dream ever since. He opened his arm and took a deep breath. Best of all, I don't think that rat, James, ever got the reward money either. These are the two horses I shipped from Scotland. I would not part with them for anything, but this one was bought and paid for right here, and your aunt has the receipt." That night, Tom told the story to the family. Finally, they were able to look at Wright Rule with more respect even though he had stolen the duke's horses. It was an eye for an eye or a dog for a horse. That night after supper, the family came out and saw Tom's horse. He had named her Henriette.

About this time, they found the school house. It was a cabin built down past the gray barn, and children of all ages went, so George could go too. The teacher was a young woman who had arrived from Scotland. Her name was Leafie Huntley and it was her relatives' cabin the Doddses had stayed in when they first came to Rossie. Leafie and her husband were from the Scottish highlands; hence, the little community was slowly becoming a tightknit Scottish society. School was out for summer break, and the children would begin again in November after the fall harvest. The family was settling in, and Thomas was happier than Helen had seen him in years. All was well except that Helen knew Jenny must be pregnant. On a hot August morning after doing the breakfast dishes, Helen asked Jenny to go for a walk with her.

"Ma, I would, but I told Leafy I would help her sew curtains for the school."

"Well, that will just have to wait then, won't it?"

"Yes, Ma, it will." They began strolling through the cornfield now high with ripe corncobs. Wright had built a wood bench in a clearing just past the field. He often came here, smoked his pipe, and whittled away listening to the sounds of the forest. Helen motioned for Jenny to sit beside her. She did not hesitate. Hesitating would just prolong the pain.

"Jenny, are you pregnant?"

"What?" Jenny exclaimed mortified that her mother would say such a thing.

"You heard me. Are you?"

"Ma, oh no, no. Why are you asking me this?"

"Because you were very sick on the ship, you had the mask, and you are putting on weight in your stomach."

"You were sick too and Tom and George and most of the passengers."

"I know, but, Jenny, if you are, you need to be thinking about the baby and not yourself. We need to get you examined by the local midwife. I heard she is good."

Jenny was stunned. Pregnant. No way. Helen shook her head and then thought, "Maybe she really doesn't know."

156

"Okay, Jenny, have you done something that could create a child?" She knew she did not want to hear the answer. Sex before marriage was a sin in the church. She would be a marked woman and ineligible for marriage.

"No, no!" Jenny cried. Tears began to stream down her face. "Oh, Ma, I am so sorry. I am so sorry. Yes, it is possible but…."

"But he asked for your hand in marriage. Why on earth did you turn him down after…."

"What?" Jenny had to focus. "Marriage?"

Ignoring Jenny's mumbling, Helen went on, "Jenny, how could you? I am so disappointed." Helen looked away. Tears burst from her eyes and trailed down her cheeks. This was a disaster, especially now that they were trying to start anew. What would everyone say?

"Ma, I don't know. I, I just love him so much. I…."

Helen finally found her voice and sobbed, "I am very disappointed in Fergus. Your father will never forgive him for this."

"Fergus?" Finally, she realized that her mother thought Fergus was the father.

"Jenny, I can't believe you did this. When were you with him in that way? When is the baby due?"

"Ma, I know. I am so sorry. I don't know. I don't even know if I am pregnant."

"Oh, you are; believe me, you are. Now everything adds up—the moods, the constant sickness, the weight gain. How could you have not known? How could I have not known?" Helen stood up, paced back and forth, stopped, and asked, "My God, Jenny, so you haven't seen a midwife or a doctor, have you?"

"No," Jenny whispered, her head hanging down. How did this happen to her? Maybe she wasn't even pregnant, but now her mother knew she had bedded someone. "I am so stupid. I know I can't be pregnant," but she touched her stomach and at that moment, she knew—the vomiting, tender breasts, irritability, and lately the sense of movement. "Oh, ma, I am so stupid. I never thought…."

"That's right, you didn't, and I should have talked with you about this, but I had no idea you would betray the church and us. We will make an appointment with a doctor over in Ogdensburg where no one knows us. Your father cannot know. He will never forgive Fergus, and since he is to be your husband, we can't have that." Helen's mind was racing. "You are probably about five months, so if you marry Fergus now, we may be able to fool the village and your father. We can call it an early birth and a miracle the baby survived."

"What? What husband? Ma, stop. I'm not marrying Fergus."

"Oh yes you are, young girl, pregnant or not. It was done when he bedded you." Jenny wanted to protest and tell the truth, but of course she could not. That would be worse than being pregnant by Fergus. They walked back to the house as Jenny's mind raced frantically trying to figure out what to do.

The next day, they hooked up the carriage and went to Ogdensburg under the pretense of shopping for sugar and flour.

"But you can get that at the local store," Thomas suggested.

"I know," Helen replied, "but we want to see this place, Ogdensburg." It was that day, September 2, 1819, that Jenny learned she was five months pregnant. She would have a Christmas baby.

On September 3, she approached Fergus with her mother's plan. Jenny realized that if she did not marry him, she would bring this down on her family and her baby. She had to accept the marriage proposal, tell Fergus the truth, and hope that he would still accept her. She met him that morning at the livery stable as he was preparing his horse.

"Fergus, good morning."

"Why, Jenny. Good morning to you. What are you doing here so early?"

"Fergus, I need to talk with you."

"Okay." Fergus dropped what he was doing and joined Jenny.

"What is it, Jenny?"

"Fergus, I know this is quite a change, but I have been thinking about your proposal."

"Yes."

"I accept."

"What? Why? Oh, my God; why does it matter? Jenny, you have made me the happiest man in the world." He encircled her in his arms and swung her around. "When, Jenny; when do you want to get married?"

"Soon, maybe next Sunday after church."

"What? Okay, then. I will talk to the preacher, I already asked your father for your hand in Scotland when I asked you the first time, but you know I am just renting a room right now. I have no home. I must tell you this; I have heard from my cousin, Jeff, who has settled north of here, and I was planning to go there."

"What? Where? You mean Jeff Rutherford."

"Yes. He is in a place called Chestertown now, but he bought land in the mountains east of there, and that is where I want to live. Jenny, I had no idea you would change your mind."

'Oh no,' she thought, 'this will not do.' Their plan did not include her leaving her family, and her heart was still breaking for John Scott. "But when, when were you going?"

"Soon, Jenny, but I can wait. We don't have to go right away. We don't have to go at all."

'Thank God,' Jenny thought, knowing she could not travel. 'You must tell him, Jenny,' a little voice kept nagging at her.

"Ah Fergus, I have something to tell you."

"Yes,"

"Ah, ah,"

"Yes, Jenny, what is it?"

"Fergus, there is no other way to say this, and when I do, I think you will not marry me, but I have to be truthful with you. I am pregnant."

"What? What did you say?"

"Fergus, I am going to have a baby."

"A baby; but we never…."

"I know. She stared into his brown eyes. They reminded her of a beautiful fawn roan and then she saw the light go out of them when he realized what she was saying."

"For God's sake, Jenny, who, whose baby are you having?"

"It is John's, John Scott, but no one knows."

"Oh my God, Walter Scott's nephew?"

"Yes."

"But." He thought back to the day after the storm when he took her there. "You bedded another who won't marry you, and now you want me to marry you? You are not the woman I thought you were. My God, you even had me take you to him. Now leave, please leave me. I can no longer look at you." By this time Jenny was sobbing so hard she could barely breathe. She turned and ran out of the stable and into the woods. She was terrified. She would be alone with a baby. She was sure her father and the church would turn her out. Contacting John Scott would be a waste of time. There was nothing he could do even if he wanted to. She had written him since arriving here. He was in Oxford continuing his education. What would she do?

She went home and immediately told her mother. "You what? You told him it was not his baby?" Helen could not believe how dense this girl seemed to be.

"Yes, ma. I had to tell him."

"Yes, maybe but after the marriage, not before." Jenny, ran to the loft sobbing hysterically. Helen went straight to Fergus.

"Fergus, I need to talk with you. I know this news was a shock to you, but I also know you love my daughter."

"Mrs. Dodds, you know?"

"Yes, I know."

"How could she do this to me?"

"I don't know, Fergus; I guess she was young, and those two were left alone in that place too much. Her father and I had no idea this was going on."

"Going on. How long was it going on?"

"Apparently, for a while during the summer months and vacations."

"Oh my God, so she is in love with him."

"I don't know if she knows what love is, Fergus, but even if she does, nothing can come of the two of them. He will graduate university and marry a woman of his class. She does not even want him to know."

"What did Thomas say?"

"He doesn't know." Fergus thought about that and knew that this plan would involve him claiming the child as his.

"I do love her, Mrs. Dodds, but that is asking a lot of me."

"I know, Fergus, but she will be shunned, and I believe Thomas may turn her out, so I am asking you to save her." Fergus agreed to think about it, and that night he prayed about it. While sitting in the little church, a realization came to him that he loved her so much that he could not let her fall into this pit of shame. She would not be eligible for marriage and who knows what would become of her in this new land. He loved her. He loved her in sickness and in health. He would protect her from wolves, bears, or anything else, so he would protect her from this.

By now, Thomas Dodds had bought a hundred acres, nearly square, on the Bay Road and contracted with George Parish to complete the payment of $2.15 per acre in seven years. He would receive his deed on April 30, 1827. He had built one cabin and was building another for his shop. Their cabin was twenty-four feet long and eighteen feet wide with one room. The floor consisted of loose puncheons. There was no hearth or fireplace, only a place for each and a banking of rude stonework against the logs at one end. At the foot of this stonework on the ground was where they built the fire with the smoke gradually escaping out of a hole in the side of the roof. There was no window, only a place cut through the log wall on the side opposite the door. Rough boards covered the roof. Thomas and Tom built an oven the second year they were there.

There was no privacy except for a curtained bed for Thomas and Helen. Therefore, if Fergus and Jenny lived with them they would have no privacy. Thomas agreed to give them a piece of land, and a month later with the help of family and friends, their little cabin was ready. Ann, who knew that John Scott was the father started a story that Fergus and Jenny had been engaged for some time before moving to Rossie, making Jenny's sudden pregnancy a little less sinful to the wagging tongues about town.

They were married in the little church at the end of town on Sunday, and Ned Elmer Walton arrived with a loud wail on Christmas Eve. He weighed nine pounds, and Fergus fell in love with him the moment he saw him. Jenny was overwhelmed with gratitude for this amazing man who took her in. She would devote her life to him though her heart would always beat for another. Thomas Dodds held his grandson for the first time, and when he looked down upon his face, he knew.

CHAPTER XV

1825

The whippoorwill zoomed past the rose bushes straight into the morning sun that was cresting over the cabin and melting the leftover frost that covered the freshly plowed fields like a winter's coat. Ann stepped out of the cabin door and headed toward the store, her red pigtails no longer flying in the wind. Now her hair was loosely secured in a bun at the nape of her neck. She was off to the general store where she worked. As she walked down the dusty street, Ann recalled their first few weeks in Rossie. She hated leaving Scotland, but now she had adjusted to this new land.

She looked over at Jenny and Fergus' cabin. Fergus was true to his word; he was a good husband to her sister. "Morning, Jen."

"Morning Ann," Jenny was sending their son, Ned, off to the little schoolhouse. "Now, no trouble, you hear? Listen to your teacher, Son."

"That's right, Ned, especially when that teacher is me," Ann laughed. She patted him on the shoulder as he walked by, his curly blond hair pushing out from under his cap. Ann taught part time at the school. "I can't believe he is seven years old now," Ann said.

"Me neither," Jenny replied, watching Ann step onto the porch and disappear through the wooden doorframe her father had built. At times Jenny still thought of her first love, but she had learned to push those thoughts away and go on. Thinking of him brought unwelcomed guilt. Fergus was good to her, and she was completely in love with little Ned. He had John's blond hair and blue eyes, but he was built stocky like her father. She and Fergus had built a home here, but Fergus still dreamed of the mountains. He missed the hills and valleys of Scotland. Last year, he had made a trip up the St. Lawrence to Lake Champlain to meet his friend Jeff in Chestertown. He learned that Jeff was married and now had a daughter and a son. Jeff took Fergus out to explore land that bordered the waters of a river called the Hudson. While there in the Pendleton settlement, Fergus, Jeff, and few other settlers bought land. It was so cheap that they could not resist the offers the landowners were making. Besides, Fergus loved this land— the perfume scent of the balsams, the roar of the swollen creeks, and the rise of the mountains peppered with green pines. He came back to Rossie more excited than Jenny had ever seen him. "Jenny, oh God, Jenny, this land, it is so beautiful with forests full of animals and waters full of fish."

"That is nice, Fergus. Maybe you can take Ned hunting there one day."

"Yes, I would, but, Jen, I would like to move there."

"Permanently?" She couldn't believe she had heard him correctly. "Fergus, our home is here. My family is here."

"I know, Lass, but we can have so much more land; they are practically giving it away to encourage settlers to come, and they say it is the most fertile land in the state. What a place for young Ned to learn."

"Learn what?" Jenny asked, her voice becoming louder.

"Uh, learn how to shoot and fish and become a man."

"He can do all that here," Jenny remarked, fear rising through her as she began to realize that her husband was serious.

"But we would be starting a new community, and when we looked out our windows, we would see the bluest, clearest water you ever saw. Jenny, you say you miss the Tweed. There are many rivers and lakes in this land, and the land I bought was so cheap."

"What? You bought? You bought land?" Jenny ran to the jar where they kept their money. Most of it was gone. "Oh, my God, Fergus, you spent the money for our next crops and the plow we were saving for."

Fergus put his arms around her. "Yes, Lass, but we will have more, and I just, I just could not stay here after seeing those mountains. It is like God gave us a little of Scotland here in this new land." Jenny began to cry and then sob as she lay her face against his shoulder. She thought back through the past seven years and all that Fergus had done for her. She knew he hated it here and would have stayed in Scotland or gone back if not for her. She realized that she was being selfish. She pulled away. "Fergus, sit down and tell me about this country you love so much." As Fergus talked, Jenny saw a light shining in his eyes she had not seen in years. He was so excited that it began to transfer to her, and she knew she would soon be in another new land starting over again; also, she was pregnant again, and Fergus did not know.

They left on April 1st. They would live in an empty cabin left by a couple who had drowned in the Hudson River, a detail Fergus did not tell his wife. They left with Ned and Ann who was so thrilled to hear that there were mountains somewhere that she was going no matter what. She found a replacement part-time teacher for the school children and prepared to leave with her sister. Helen and Thomas strongly objected to the move. Helen thought the timing foolish because Jenny was pregnant. "My Lord, Jenny, you can't go off into the wilderness carrying a child."

"Ma, I did it when we left Scotland traveling thousands of miles. This is nothing compared to that."

"Distance, yes, but where you are going is wild territory, and for God's sake you haven't even told Fergus you are pregnant."

"I will, Ma, after we are on our way. He is so happy that I don't want to influence his decision by telling him. I will tell him on the way, though."

Helen knew that once Jenny made up her mind about something there was no changing it. "I don't like this at all, Jen, but at least Ann is with you to help." Helen also knew her daughter, Ann, was a capable girl inside or outside of the house. She could tramp for miles on land, hit anything she aimed at, and come home and bake a loaf of bread.

"That's right, Ma, and Jeff and Celia Rutherford are meeting us. They have children, so Celia will help, and I am sure there is a midwife in the community."

There were tearful goodbyes, and George vowed that when he was old enough he would come too. Robert wanted to go, but Da needed him and Tom on the farm, so for the first time, he and Ann would be separated. He would miss her terribly. "I will come back and see all of you," Ann said as she gave Robert a hug, both sobbing like children. Mary was already engaged to one of the Dalzell boys. "Will you be able to come to my wedding next spring?"

"Oh, Mary, I will absolutely be here," Jenny assured her as she climbed up on the wagon. It was a balmy Tuesday morning when the wagon rolled out of Rossie with all their possessions. They headed north to meet the steamship that would take them back up the mighty St. Lawrence and east to a wilderness populated by bear, moose, panther, coyote, wolves, and a few humans.

And so began another trip on the St. Lawrence. They boarded the ship at Waddington and sailed to Montreal where once again Jenny entered the store where she had met Henriette Desautels. When she stepped in and looked up, she saw a young girl who looked like Henriette, the girl Tom was so smitten with on the trip over. Jenny walked up to the counter and asked, "Do the Desautels still own this store?"

"Yes, I am Lucille Desautels. My brother and I own the store."

"I am asking because I met a woman named Henriette when we came here from Scotland. Her father owned the store."

169

"Yes, she is my sister, but they have moved to the United States."

"Really?"

"Yes, my mother, father, one brother, and Henriette moved to a place on the St. Lawrence River."

"Do you know the name of the settlement?"

"Ah, yes, yes. I have a post from them." She rummaged under the counter and came out with an envelope. "Let me see. Oh, yes, it is from a place called Waddington."

"Waddington." Jenny looked up at Fergus. "Oh, my gosh, they live only a few miles from my family," Jenny exclaimed. "I will write to tell them to look them up."

"Very good; very good," Lucille said, "and where do you go now?"

"We are going to the place over the border called Deer Hunting Country on the map," Fergus replied.

"Oh, oh, I see," Lucille replied, turning quickly, and busying herself with folding and rearranging items in the store. Jenny bought some thread and turned to leave. "Do be careful."

"Oh, thank you," Jenny replied, noticing what she thought was a worried look on Lucille's face. Out on the street, Jenny mentioned it to Fergus. "Fergus, why did Lucille look so worried? I know there is always danger traveling these routes, but is there something else I should know about?"

"Yes, I saw that too," Ann remarked, looking at Fergus.

"Ah, women; I am sure Lucille is worried about our traveling alone with a child, but I have my gun and knife right here." He patted his knife and put his arm around her. "Jenny, I will protect you and our son with my life."

"I know. I just pray that you don't have to."

"Don't you worry. Jeff has told me all I need to know. We will be fine. By the way," he chuckled, "I would think you would be writing to your brother to tell him his Henriette is only a horse ride away from him."

Jenny's thoughts turned to her brother and she smiled. "Yes, that is exactly what I am going to do." Now, all she could think about was going to their room and posting a letter to Tom telling him that the woman he thought he would never see again was living right next to him.

The next morning, they boarded the stage and headed southeast to St-Jean-sur-Richelieu, a port on the Richelieu River. This river would take them back across the border where they would eventually take a boat down Lake Champlain to a place called Whitehall. As the stage bumped along on the barely passable road, Ann saw smoke billowing up into the sky. She knew these were Indian camps and wondered if they would be friendly. They had not met many Native Americans in Rossie except for the few who came down from Canada to sell their baskets and pelts.

Finally, after being tossed around for hours, they reached the port where the last steam ship had already left. Not wanting to use what little money they had, Jenny asked if they could sleep on the stage in the livery. The driver agreed to their request if Fergus took care of the horses and cleaned the stage, which he gladly agreed to do.

The next morning, they boarded a horse-powered ferry that would shuttle them to Whitehall; there they could buy a horse and wagon to take them to the settlement of Chestertown where Jeff and Celia would be waiting for them, they hoped. Postal service was not reliable, so although Fergus had posted a letter, there was no time for Jeff to write back. Fergus just had to hope the letter made it and Jeff and Celia would be there.

Sadly, upon boarding the ferry that took them down the newly built Champlain Canal, they had to part with several of their items, such as the dishes Jenny received from her parents for her wedding. She managed to hold onto her silverware, and Fergus kept his joiner tools. He would need them to build their cabin. The horses yoked together on each end of the deck fascinated Ned. As the animals walked a treadmill, they powered the paddles. Ann, the only other family member who knew Jenny was pregnant was constantly at her side asking about her health.

The navigator spoke only French, which was a little disconcerting because they had to trust that this rough-looking character was not charging them too much money; however, they were in a strange country without protection, so Fergus paid the fare. From the little French Jenny remembered from school, the captain told them they would be at their destination the next day.

Throughout this grueling journey, Jenny was relieved that she was not getting too sick. She estimated that she was about ten weeks along and was surprised she was not sick on the stagecoach ride. She did not look forward to the twenty-five-mile wagon ride she would have to endure from Whitehall to Chestertown, but so far all was well. Their money was getting low, but Jeff had assured Fergus he had a job for him, and there was plenty of game in the woods, so they would be okay.

They were halfway to their destination when the pains started. Jenny had just finished handing out the sandwiches she had made for them. She bent over to put the remaining jars in her bag when a sharp pain in her stomach forced her to double over and scream. Fergus and Ned ran to her. "Jenny, what is it? What's wrong?" Fergus asked as he put his arm around her waist and set her down on the cot.

"Ma!" Ned cried. He ran in search of Ann, found her, and told her his mom was hurting. Ann raced with Ned to her sister. By now, Jenny had caught her breath and looked up at their worried faces.

"I'm okay now. False alarm. Guess it was the food."

"You look tired, honey, and why would the food do this? We ate the same thing as you."

"I don't know, Fergus, but if you just leave me and let me rest, I'm sure I will be fine."

"Okay, Jen, but I will be back to check on you in a few minutes." They left her alone, and Jenny's mind began to race. Should she tell Fergus now? He was so worried about them on this trip. They would be in Whitehall tomorrow. She would tell him then. This was just a cramp. She had them with Ned at times, but she did not have them this early in her pregnancy. She would be okay. She just needed sleep.

"Jen, you need to tell Fergus. It is not right," Ann chided. "If you don't tell him soon, I will. This is ridiculous. Your reasoning about him not going because of this baby is no longer true. Why do you keep on lying? I don't get it."

"I don't know, Ann, it just hasn't felt right to tell him. I promise I will tell him tonight. I need to rest now."

"Very well. You sleep. I'll keep an eye on Ned."

Jenny was asleep before Ann got out of the room, but she woke up to Ned's high-pitched voice screaming, "Ma, wake up! We have to go."

"Go where?"

"We have to go on another boat."

"What?" Jenny slowly pulled herself up from the cot. She was still tired. Her body was so heavy she could hardly climb the ladder to the deck. Upon emerging from the hold, she faced a horrific scene she would relive over and over for the rest of her life. There before her was Fergus, arms tied behind his back, face covered in bruises, looking at her with such sadness that it broke her heart. Standing beside him were the captain and his mate with guns pointed at all of them.

"What? What is happening?" Jenny whispered finally taking in the scene before her.

"Ma, they're robbing us!" Ned sobbed. "Da tried to fight them when they asked him for all his money. They hit him so many times; I was scared and ran and got you." He was shaking, sobbing, and

174

gasping for breath between his words. Jenny looked at the captain and then at the little boat he had lowered into the water.

In broken English, the mate said, "You go on this or be killed." Jenny could not believe her ears.

"You are making us get off into this little wooden boat?"

"Get off. Yes."

"But how?"

Fergus spoke through swollen bloody lips, "Jenny, they are robbers. I am so sorry. I didn't know. Get in the boat, or they will kill us all. We are only about five miles from Whitehall. We can make it."

"In an old wooden rowboat?"

"For God's sake, Jen, get in the damn boat!" Ann yelled as she pushed her sister toward the boat. She knew that these men would just as soon kill them as let them go. It was going to be whichever was easier for them, and if Jen didn't shut up and do what she was told, shutting her up with a bullet in her head would prove easier for these men.

"No more time. Get in or I kill your man." He put the gun against Fergus' head.

"Please let us get our food," Jenny begged. "Please." They allowed her to get some food. She grabbed the bag and the money she had tucked away in the pocket. She took their Bible, water, and as much food as she could gather. She grabbed a couple of blankets and headed for the front deck followed by the mate. She did not even know their names. It dawned on her that the captain and first mate had not introduced themselves, and now she knew why-- so they could not be identified. Other passengers had boarded, but Whitehall was the last stop so they were the only ones left on the boat. She tried to plead with the mate, but he pretended to only understand a few words. With the gun still pointed at Fergus' head, Jenny, Ann, and Ned climbed into the boat. They sat looking up waiting for the captain to untie Fergus, so he could climb in the boat. The captain hit Fergus over the head so hard he fell to the floor of the ship. Then he and the mate rolled him over the side. Fergus fell with his head and shoulders in the wooden boat while the rest of him hung in the water. The boat listed heavily to the right, and Fergus began to slip into the deep waters of Lake Champlain. Jenny and Ann grabbed him and tried desperately to pull him in; only half of him was in, and the rowboat rocked dangerously.

"Please, please help us!" Ned screamed at the robbers, tears streaming down his face.

"Don't leave us!" Jenny screamed, her screams filled the empty air as the ferryboat slowly pulled away from them. "Fergus, Fergus, wake up!" she cried. She looked over at Ned. He was sitting, staring, perched like a statue on the front seat. "Ned, get over here. Help me pull your father up." His mother's pleas stirred him from shock, but the three of them could not pull Fergus up into the boat.

"There is only one way to get him in here," Ann shouted, "I have to go into the lake and push him up while you two pull him."

"Absolutely not, Ann," Jenny objected, "that water is freezing. You will get...." Before she could finish, Ann had jumped in.

She swam in front of Fergus, grabbed his legs, and yelled, "Now you two, pull!" As Ann pushed, Ned and Jenny pulled on Fergus' shoulders, and finally they got him over the side and into the boat. Ann climbed back in, got the knife she always carried in her boot, and cut the ropes on his hands. He was bleeding from a large gash on the back of his head. Jenny ripped off a piece of her dress, wiped the wound clean using the lake water, and wrapped the blanket around his shivering body. Next, she looked down and saw the oars attached to the side of the boat. She had never paddled a boat, but she soon found out that Ann had paddled a couple of times on the Tweed.

"Oh my God, Ann, you went in a boat on the Tweed?"

"Yup, me and Sam Hamilton."

"For God's sake, if Da had found out he would have spanked you good."

"I know, but he didn't. Good thing I did it though, right? Anyway, give me those oars." She said with a sad grin. She seated herself in the middle seat, grabbed the oars, and began to pull backwards, red hair stuck in strands to the side of her face. Jenny stared at her sister. She was always amazed at Annie's fearlessness and strange sense of humor. As the boat began to move, Jenny looked over at Ned and saw that he was staring again. "Ned, honey, please come up front and watch for any signs of life along the shore."

"Ok, Ma."

Ann, seeing what was going on with Ned said, "Okay, Ned, and then we will change positions when my arms get tired. You will have to row."

"Ok, I can do that," Ned replied coming out of his silence and scouring the shoreline for movement, smoke, or any other sign of life.

177

Soon they were making progress down the canal. Jenny was praying for another ferry to come by, but it was getting dark and she knew most of them were in port by now. She had no idea where Whitehall was. They paddled, rested, and scanned the forest for a cabin, smoke, or anything moving, but all they saw for miles were giant green trees nestled between the bare-branched hardwoods. Jenny thought about how on another day she and Fergus would have loved seeing this colorful painting reflected in the clear blue waters of this amazing river. However, this day was not for seeing beauty; it was for tending to Fergus and making sure her family survived. She was about to give up and have them sleep in the boat for the night when Ned hollered, "Smoke, I see smoke!" he pointed toward the eastern shoreline. Jenny and Ann knew it could be fog as the nights were cool, and they remembered how the thick fog rolled in at the start of their trip on the north end of Lake Champlain. It had been so dense they could not even see each other on the ship if they were more than eight feet away.

"I think it is probably fog, dear," Jenny said as she hugged Ned to her.

"No, I think he is right; I think it is smoke." Ann said excitedly.

As they got closer to shore, Jenny realized it was smoke. By now Ned and Ann had mastered rowing. They turned the little boat left and headed toward the smoke, a small prick of fear pierced Jenny's mind as she remembered seeing the smoke on the river and listening to the stories in Scotland about the savages in the new land.

Chapter XVI

They heard stones scraping against the bottom of the boat as they nosed it between two boulders and onto a small stretch of rocky shore. They had the slim light of a crescent moon to guide them. They did not know what time it was or where they were. However, they did know that where there is smoke there are people. They pulled the boat up on shore as far as they could and once again tried to wake Fergus. They could not wake him. Jenny knew he was barely breathing, but he was alive. He would not be for long if she did not get help. They could no longer see the smoke because the trees shot up around them like towers blocking their view.

"That's okay," Ann, said, "I've got it." She ran to the tallest white pine tree and began climbing.

"Oh, Ann, do be careful," Jenny cautioned.

"You know I've been climbing since I was three years old. This is an easy one." In a few minutes, she shouted down, "I see it! I see the smoke! It's that way." She pointed straight out away from the river. By the time Ann dropped to the ground, Jenny had put her math and geography skills to work.

"Okay, we were headed south so we are on the east side of the river; we will go east in the morning. Let's gather some pine boughs and make camp here. It is cold but if we huddle together.... Wait, we can't. Oh my God, we can't. Fergus won't last that long. We need to get help tonight."

"I know, I know," Ann whispered, putting her arm around her sister, "but we can't just go off into this wilderness. What if we fall in a pond or a hole?" She walked over to the edge of the woods. "Jenny, I can't even find a deer trail in this blackness. We are going to have to gather around Fergus and pray that he can make it until it's light. We have the two blankets and each other." She bent down and started unfolding the blankets. "We will use...." Suddenly a horrific scream broke through the crisp night air. Ann turned and saw Jenny with her hand over her mouth pointing into the bushes. "Jenny, what?" Then she saw him too. Standing under the bent white birch tree was a figure. It was so dark that she could not make out what or who it was.

Ned ran to Jenny; she pulled him tight to her, both frozen in place. Ann finally saw what she thought was an image of a man. She gathered enough courage to mutter out, "Hello, who's there?" She wanted to ask what he was doing here. She wanted the knife that she had left in the boat. 'How stupid,' she thought. 'We have one weapon and cannot use it.' The man came forward. He ducked down to avoid a branch, and when he stood up they saw he was wearing a strange looking pointed hood and a long cloak. He did not look like any person they had ever seen, and they were frightened.

"He's an Indian," Ned said. "He looks like the ones in my school books."

"I wonder if he speaks English," Ann said, regaining a little courage.

"Do you speak English?" Ned asked.

"Ned, no," Jenny chided, "you might make him mad." She pushed Ned behind her.

"Yes," the Indian said.

"What?" Ann asked, completely forgetting what Ned had asked.

"Yes, I speak English."

"You do. Oh my, you do. Oh, my God, Jenny, he speaks English!" Ann was so excited she forgot their whole frightening situation. "Sir, ah, mister, do you live near here?"

"Yes."

"Where the smoke is coming from?" Ann pointed in the direction she saw the smoke.

"Yes."

"I am Ann. This is my sister, Jenny, and her son, Ned. His father is still in the boat. He is injured."

"I am Patrick."

"Patrick," Ann said, amazed that this man had an Irish name, but she didn't care. If he didn't kill them, he might be able to help. She explained to him what had happened, and he understood most of it. He went to the boat and looked at Fergus.

"Very sick. This man is very sick. We need to bring him to our village to help him. It is not far." He picked Fergus up and threw him over his shoulder. "Come." Jenny did not think it was a clever idea to go off into the woods with this savage.

Jenny looked at Ann. Her voice trembled as she warned, "Ann, we may never come out again. We don't know what these people will do. Remember what they told us back home. They rape the women, kill the men, and raise the children as their own. We cannot go."

Ann stared at Patrick as he stood there with Fergus. Granted, he was intimidating, but what choice did they have? "Well, Jenny, he could have killed us all by now, and I am freezing. Besides, Fergus may have a chance if they can help him, and if they are going to kill us, they will do it here or there. At least there, Fergus has a chance."

Jenny and Ned agreed with Ann's reasoning and motioned for Patrick to go on. However, even with Fergus over his shoulder, they had difficulty keeping up with Patrick. Finally, they saw lights flickering through the pines as they entered a clearing in the woods that opened into an Abenaki village. "Wow," Ned said, "just like in the books." The village had many wigwams in all different shapes forming a circle. "Look, Ma; it's a longhouse!" On the far perimeter of the village was a longhouse made of logs. They were at once surrounded by men and women who offered them warm blankets and food.

"I take this man to our healer," Patrick said as he began to walk toward the longhouse.

"No!" Jenny screamed and tried to pull Fergus off the Indian's shoulder.

Ann grabbed Jenny's arm. "Let him go, Jen. Maybe this healer is a doctor."

"You mean a witch doctor," Jenny cried as she let go and ran after Fergus. She entered the building behind Patrick. An older man with no hair in front and two feathers jutting out from a ponytail in back greeted Patrick. They put Fergus on a platform covered in blankets. The man put something greasy on Fergus' forehead and covered him with blankets. It was hot inside and the heat was comforting to Jenny. Patrick came over to her and ushered her out. "My father must work on him now alone with the spirits."

"Your father? But, I want to be with him. I need...."

"No, it is not allowed. Please come. You need help too. You are very cold."

Jenny turned and walked out of the longhouse with Patrick. Soft fires burned in front of wigwams circled throughout the village. A young woman brought Ann a leather shirt, skirt, and shawl; Ann was shaking so badly she could barely stand. The same woman led them into a dome-shaped wigwam and then gave them blankets and a warm soup-like food to eat while they sat around a fierce fire.

Before long, the healer and Patrick came to their wigwam. The old man spoke to Patrick in Abenaki, and Patrick translated to the three of them that Fergus was badly hurt and might not make it through the night. Patrick's father would stay with Fergus through the night. Jenny wanted to stay with Fergus, but the healer seemed upset by this. Patrick intervened and explained that his father would watch Fergus all night in the longhouse that he shared with his wife and daughter. Though Jenny wanted desperately to be with him, she understood and was grateful that this man was willing to stay the night with her husband. Patrick left, and the young woman laid out three thick bear hides for them to sleep on. She covered them with colorful blankets; within minutes, they were asleep.

The next morning when they opened their eyes, Jenny and Ann saw a white woman and an Indian girl standing over them. "Hello, I am Evelyn, Patrick's mother and this is my daughter, Gizos. My husband, Namito, has been treating your husband all night," the woman said gently as she glanced toward Patrick who was entering the tent. "Your husband is asking for you."

"Who?" Jenny was still groggy and adjusting to where she was. She was surprised to hear English and see another white woman.

"Your husband. He wishes to see you."

"My husband. He is awake? Oh, Lord, he is awake!"

"Yes, but my father says he can do no more for him, so he may go to see his ancestors," the young Indian girl cautioned.

"What? Go to see what?" Jenny was confused and so happy to hear that Fergus was awake that she jumped up and ran to the longhouse. As soon as she entered, the scent of spices and wood smoke engulfed her. Fergus was still lying on the platform covered with a black bearskin. When Jenny kneeled and took his hand, he did not move. She looked questioningly at Namito; she was about to ask if he was awake when Fergus whispered her name.

"Jenny."

"Yes, Fergus. Oh, you had me scared to death, but you are awake now."

"Jenny, listen to me. Oh, Jen, I have always loved you. I never wanted to leave you, and I surely did not think it would be this soon."

184

"What? What are you saying? Fergus, they are going to take care of you. You are going to get better."

"No, Jenny, I am not." He began to cough. He coughed until Jenny thought he would die. She lifted his head up as far as she could, and the hacking finally stopped. "Jen, I know you loved another, but you have given me nothing but love all these years."

"Oh, Fergus, that was years ago…."

"I know, and you left John never telling him he had a son. Tell him, Jenny, you must tell him."

"But, he is your son."

"That he is, but a man should know his son. Find him, Jenny."

"What?"

"Find John. He is close."

"What? What do you mean, Fergus?" The hacking began again. He groaned and muttered incoherently. The fever was so high she could feel the heat rising from his body.

She lowered his head, looked into his sad brown eyes, and said, "Fergus, that is nonsense. You will make it." Ned and Ann walked in with Evelyn.

"Ned," Fergus whispered extending his hand out to Ned. While Ned held his father's hand, Evelyn explained that Fergus had caught influenza and that there was no medicine for that sickness. Namito could not save him. Jenny hugged Ned to her and held onto Fergus' hand. Ann stood beside them.

Just as the sun was dipping down over the mountains, Fergus let go of Jenny's hands for the last time. "No, Fergus, no, please, wake up. Wake up," she cried.

Ann gently tugged at her sister's arm. "Jenny, he's gone. You have to let go." Jenny stood up and put her arms around Ann and Ned, and they sobbed uncontrollably until Gizos told them that her father said that Fergus was not gone; rather, his spirit had gone to join his ancestors.

"It is a time for celebration, not sadness," Gizos translated from her father. Jenny could not think of anything to celebrate. Here she was out in this Godforsaken land alone with these strange people. The man she had learned to love was gone, and her plans for carrying on were gone.

That evening in front of the campfire, Jenny looked at Ann, "Oh, Ann, what are we to do? We do not have enough money to go back, and we don't know what is ahead. I don't even know where we are or how to get to this Chestertown place Fergus was taking us to."

"The Abenaki must know the way," Ann suggested, "maybe Patrick can take us." Ann was right; Patrick, Gizos, and their father hunted and fished all through that area. Gizos related that she and Patrick had fished with their father near this land.

Jenny knew she could not carry Fergus out, and so with the help of the Abenaki, on June 2, 1825, she buried him under a giant red spruce tree that towered over the village. Afterward, Patrick carved a cross in the trunk of the tree. Jenny thought this to be equivalent to the stones they placed in their cemeteries. She later learned that it marked

186

the grave of an Indian, but they made an exception for such a brave warrior as Fergus who was willing to journey to this new land.

That night, Evelyn visited them in their tent. "How did you come to live here, and where are you from?" Jenny asked. Evelyn related that she was from Ireland and her parents and sister contacted Typhoid on the ship bringing them to New York. They made it to land and the Abenaki rescued them. The only survivor was Evelyn. She grew up with Namito; they fell in love, married, and she stayed. She helped her husband in his medicine practice. She said that most of the Abenaki people had been forced into Maine and Canada by the white settlers, but a few tribes had stayed.

"But don't you miss the way you used to live?"

"No, I was a child when I came here, and they took me in. I love living in nature. I go to sleep listening to the creek and wake up listening to the woodpeckers, and mockingbirds. I also teach the children, and now most of them speak English and Abenaki."

"But your husband only speaks Abenaki? You did not teach him?"

Evelyn laughed, "Oh yes, he does speak English, but he is a typical Abenaki and likes to remain private, so he only speaks English to his family or in an emergency. Now, you won't let him know I told you, will you?" She smiled at Jenny.

"No," Jenny replied, "I certainly will not."

Now, I leave you to rest. You have a long day tomorrow." Jenny thanked her once again and fell asleep to the sound of the fast-moving waters of the creek swollen by the spring rains.

The next morning Jenny knelt before the beautiful burial tree and said her last goodbye to Fergus. Then, she gathered Ann and Ned, and they said their goodbyes to Namito, Evelyn, and several other friends they had made. Gizos and Patrick would take the family to Whitehall where they could board the stagecoach for Chestertown. Jenny thanked Namito for trying to save her husband. He told her in Abenaki that Fergus was in the spirit world now watching over her. Evelyn translated. He also whispered to Ann just before she turned to leave, "We will meet again." He spoke in English.

Ann smiled and looked surprised but nodded her head. She wondered if he meant here on earth or in the spirit world. She did not plan on coming back here. She had said her goodbyes to Fergus and coming back would bring sadness. Besides, she would never have reason to return here. She thanked him again, turned, and headed west toward Whitehall.

After an hour, Jenny and Ned were lagging, but Ann was keeping stride with Patrick and Gizos. Ann looked around in amazement at the deep brown stalks of feathery ferns with fronds so many shades of green. There was bracken that stood up on spindly legs and waved their leaves as if to beckon her to their poisonous lair: so beautiful; so potentially dangerous. Then, there were light green ferns bunched together as if a squadron ready for battle. Chipmunks and squirrels were racing up the giant oaks and maples as she breathed in the aroma of the balsam trees. They rounded a curve, and there was a magnificent red spruce tree with its giant roots wrapped around a glacier-thrown rock. Ann felt the thrill of danger always present

188

around the next curve or over the next hill. She loved this land and vowed that she would live in these forests and walk these trails. She hoped that Whitehall was like this.

As they moved along, Ann talked with Gizos. They were close to the same age and shared hunting and fishing stories. Gizos told Ann how she had made the deerskin skirt, vest, and boots she was wearing. Ann could not wait to settle in, hunt her own deer, and make clothes from the hide. During the hike, Patrick told Ann that he was named after his mother's father. He had his mother's green eyes and fairer skin color, but he and Gizos had the same straight black hair Ann had seen in Namito's ponytail.

They reached Whitehall around noon. They thanked Gizos and Patrick and asked them to visit them in their new place sometime. Patrick told them that during fall hunting, they would find them. "Thank you for everything," Jenny said; "you saved our lives." Ned and Ann also thanked them. Patrick said something in Abenaki, which later turned out to be "May spirit be with you," turned, and disappeared quickly and silently between the black-trunked trees of his magnificent homeland.

Gail Huntley

CHAPTER XVII

J enny stepped out of the forest and into the main street of Whitehall. How would she manage? What would they do? Her father or Fergus had always secured lodging and food.

"Well, we need to find a place to stay," Ann chimed in. "I asked Patrick and Gizos, and they mentioned someone named Joseph who owned an inn, so let's look."

"Okay," Jenny replied. She still had the money she had hidden away; it wasn't much, but it would help. They walked down Main Street, passing a general store, a livery, and a barber shop, before coming to another large building with black ash baskets hanging outside. An old man was on the porch making baskets.

"I'm going to ask him where the inn is," Ann said.

"No, Ann," Jenny scolded, cautioning her about speaking to strangers, but Ann had already approached the old man.

"Mister, do you know where the Joseph Inn is?"

"Ann, I'm sure he doesn't speak English," Jenny said, embarrassed by her sister's bold behavior. This man was obviously from one of the Indian tribes, probably Abenaki.

"Sure do. It's right here. Come with me." He got up slowly and led them through the open door into a room with a counter. "Elizabeth, we got customers." Soon a woman with shoulder length gray hair and deep brown eyes came into the room.

"You need a room for the night?"

"Yes," Jenny said, "but how much?"

"Well we only have three rooms, and two are taken, so you would all have to use the same room."

"That is fine," Jenny said, "how much?" The price was one dollar. Jenny paid it, and they all went to the room. It was small but bigger than what they had in Scotland, so they were content. Now they had to find food. They walked over to the general store, bought cheese and bread, walked down to the creek, filled their containers with water, and ate. The robbers had taken all their supplies, so they had to eat sparingly. That night after Ned was asleep, Jenny asked Ann if she thought she would ever see the people who helped them again.

"I hope so. Patrick said he would be back. He said he will visit me in Chestertown."

"It seems he said a lot to you. I didn't even know he spoke English that well."

"Well, he does," Ann replied, seeing his face, and remembering the depth of his emerald green eyes.

The next morning, they arrived at the livery, bought their tickets, boarded, and began the ride to Chestertown. During the trip, Ann sat up front with the driver, whose name was Dan Wheeler. She asked him if he had ever heard of the Rutherfords.

"Oh, yes ma'am. They have a farm and make the best spruce beer in the country. Jeff Rutherford has quite a business going. He

192

drives this stage sometimes on my time off. Hard-working chap. Made a name for himself in these parts. Are you the ones coming from Rossie he's been expecting? I believe it was Fergus, Fergus Walton, though I'm guessing you ain't Fergus Walton."

"No, no, Fergus was my sister's husband. He was killed on the way." Ann put her head down as a tear squeaked out of her eye and trailed down her cheek.

"Oh, so sorry, ma'am. I didn't know or wouldn't have asked."

"It was terrible. Some horrible men took all our possessions and killed Fergus. They posed as boat pilots, got us on the boat, and robbed us. They beat Fergus unconscious and then tossed us all in an old wooden rowboat. He eventually died. We buried him at an Abenaki camp." Dan listened, shaking his head.

"So sorry. Yup, we been having some problems on the river with those pirates. So sorry they found you, ma'am."

"I didn't even know there were still pirates. Oh, I'm Ann."

"Dan here. Well, Ann, I suppose they don't think of themselves as pirates, but they steal and even kill sometimes. Hate to say it, but you're lucky they put you in a boat. They've been known to dump people overboard."

"Oh, Lord, I can't even think of that. Are there many bad men around here like that?" She was now beginning to fear that many of the men around these parts were devoid of any morals or conscience.

"Well, I ain't, Ann, and most of us ain't. Most people around these parts are good hard-working people trying to make a living. Don't let those buggers scare you off." They chatted the rest of the

193

way, and though Ann carried on with the conversation, her mind kept going back over the faces of those criminals. Somehow, some way, she would see justice served. She closed her hand on the rifle she carried by her side and touched the knife hidden inside her boot. In the aftermath of their ordeal, she had left hers in the boat. Patrick had promised to go back and look for it but gave her one of his in the meantime.

Twice she bounced so far out of her seat that had she not been hanging onto the rails, she would have been tossed out. There were tree ruts and rocks all along the dirt trail just wide enough for the stagecoach to pass.

They reached Chestertown before noon. Jenny could barely move by the time the vehicle stopped. They had to stop the stage twice because she was sick. She feared for her baby because the ride was so bumpy. Looking out the window of the stage as it pulled to a stop, she saw what looked like a general store. Wheels and harnesses hung outside on the wall along with various kinds of pelts. Under the pelts were bins of onions, potatoes, and other vegetables. A man with black curly hair, a long black beard, and a pipe stood in front of the log door. A woman in a gray dress and bonnet holding a toddler stood beside him.

The man hollered, "Hey, Dan, you got 'em?"

"Sure do," Dan replied, as he let the reins down and hopped from the driver's seat of the stage. Ann hopped off the stage and walked with Dan up to the man and woman. "Well, I guess you two know each other," Dan said. Jenny looked out the window and saw the stocky man with black hair and black beard. He wore a deerskin jacket and tall moccasin boots that ended just below his knees. He was smiling, and his white teeth shone like snow against his dark skin.

Jenny leaned over and shouted out the window. "Jeff! Is that you?"

"Are you? No, it can't be," the man said.

"Yes, it is," Jenny yelled. Jeff ran to the stage, opened the door, and let Jenny out. They hugged.

"Jenny, you made it. Oh, my Lord, and the redhead, that is little pigtail Annie Ann? Lord, you are late. Fergus had said the day before yesterday. When you didn't show by this morning, I sent someone out to see if Dan had picked anyone up. He came back and told me he picked the Waltons up in Whitehall this morning, so we came to wait."

"Yes, this is Annie," Jenny said smiling, holding back the urge to vomit one more time.

"And who is the young man?" Jeff asked as Ned climbed out of the stage.

"Ned, meet Jeff Rutherford," Jenny said. "Jeff is from our hometown in Scotland."

"Welcome Ned."

"Thank you." He and Ann exited the coach and stood by Jenny.

"It is so good to see you, Jeff, but we were worried when we didn't hear from any of you for so long."

"Our ship was damaged, and they had to send for another, so our trip took months and Ma got sick, so we were waylaid in Canada for some time tending to her. She had a bad fever and could not write, and

Da doesn't write. I know I should have written, but I was trying to work every minute as we were desperate for money."

"So sorry. Your mother. How is she?"

"Good now. They are living with her relatives in Maine where Da has a thriving blacksmith business. He learned the trade from his brother-in-law. I met my wife, Celia, on the ship and moved here to her hometown." He turned back to Celia who was standing in front of the store. He motioned her to join them. "Celia, meet Jenny, Ann, and Ned.

"Hello, Welcome to our town."

Jeff turned to Ned, "Your father and I are best friends. Jen, where is he? Is he bringing a wagon with your supplies?"

Ned looked at his mother and then put his head down, "No, Sir, he died."

Jenny put her arm around him and pulled him close. "Jeff, Fergus died on the trip here. It is a long story, and I will tell you later."

"What? My God! Fergus is dead. Oh Lord, no" Jeff lamented, turning his head, and taking a deep gasp. Celia put her arms around her husband, looked at Jenny, and said, "My goodness, I am so sorry. He has been so looking forward to seeing his friend. This is horrible news, but you must be dusty and exhausted, so please, come into the house and rest."

Jeff found his voice and invited them in, putting his hand on Ned's shoulder as they made their way down the street to the Rutherford house.

Celia noticed that Jenny's face was extremely white. Glancing again she knew why. Jenny was pregnant. After four children, Celia knew the signs. "Our house is within walking distance from the store and the church. Jeff and Dan will bring your things."

"We have no things," Ned interrupted, "because they all got stole."

"That's right," Ann chimed in, "so at least we have nothing to carry." On the way, Jenny explained to Jeff and Celia how they were robbed of all their possessions including most of their money.

"I am afraid we have only a pittance left to pay you."

"Pay? Oh, heavens no, dear, you will not pay. You are from Jeff's hometown, and you are friends. Friends don't pay. Please come along with me, and we will talk no more about paying." Celia looked at Jenny. "Well, I think we are about the same size, so you can wear something of mine. Ann, I think Sadie is your size, and Ned, our Isaac is a couple years older than you, so I'm sure I can fix you up with clothes."

"Just to let you know, I don't wear dresses so if it is all the same, I can wash these trousers and dry them," Ann piped up.

"Ann!" Jenny whispered, "Stop; you will take what they have."

"I will not, Jen," Ann whispered back.

Jenny turned her face away from Celia and shushed Ann again. She could see that Celia was surprised by the way Ann dressed, even though she tried not to show it.

"Celia, Ann and I can help you with the children and the housework, and Ned can help cut and pile wood," Jenny offered.

"That would be wonderful. These children are a handful, and when are you due?"

"What? But how...."

Celia smiled and said, "How do I know? I know because I've done it four times. Believe me, I know." Celia laughed. Jenny felt the heaviness lift a little when she heard the joy in this woman's laughter. It was at that point that Ned learned he was to have brother or sister, and he was elated. They met Jeff, Jr. Sadie, Isaac, and Ernie Rutherford.

They all found places to sleep in the Rutherford house. Early the next morning, Ann grabbed her bow and met up with Dan, who took her hunting. They brought home fish and meat while Ned got a job cleaning out the stagecoaches.

Jenny enrolled Ned in school and though crowded in the two-room log cabin, they managed. It reminded Jenny of Scotland. It reminded her of her ma and da and the trips along the river to sneak away with John Scott. When she was alone walking under the white arch of the stone bridge at the edge of town or in her bed at night she allowed herself to remember. She felt guilty when she thought of John's blond hair and blue eyes. She felt like a bad person thinking of him instead of Fergus. She loved Fergus, but when her thoughts roamed free they went to that room in SandyKnowe where she knowingly and willingly abandoned herself to love's passion with John Scott.

Chapter XVIII

1830

O n a Tuesday morning in December, with the wind and snow whipping at his face, John Scott entered the rugged mountains of New York State. John's Oxford University days were over. He had continued to be a disappointment to his wealthy parents. He left Oxford before graduating because he could not fit into the stuffy atmosphere of his heritage. He loved the outdoors and had lived with his uncle who was now Sir Walter Scott since he had received the title, Baron, from King George IV. John was glad that he had spent that time with his uncle because a few years later, the man he loved and admired passed on, and John's father inherited SandyKnowe and Abbotsford House.

When John quit Oxford, his father disinherited him and banned him from his home and Sir Walter's estate. Sir Walter had left John a small sum of money, but since he was no longer the wealthy son of a baron, he no longer had ties to the land or an education with skills for employment. He began reading American newspapers and talking with relatives whose families had migrated to the new country. Then, he wrote to his cousin, Robert Scott, who was in Hammond, New York. Robert wrote back telling John about the rolling hills and forests of

Hammond. He also wrote about the great forests in the north that reminded him of the Scottish Highlands. He told John that this was wild and dangerous country where you had to hunt and fish for food and the villages were barely inhabited. Since John had little experience in anything except hunting and fishing, which he did with Uncle Walter, wild, dangerous country sounded good to him. He was used to being alone and became excited at the idea of doing something he and Uncle Walter had done together. Those were the best days of his life. He recalled riding on the back of Covenanter with his uncle shooting his first deer and laughing when his uncle described some of the strange people he knew.

Today, John stood in front of this giant wonderland of American woods listening to the silence of the snow. A white blanket stretched for miles in front of him peppered by pine branches hanging like giant, weighted hands. He already loved this land. Why had he not come here before? He knew why. He knew that when he placed his foot on this land called America, his heart would race, his breath would catch, and memories of her would flood over him. He thought he could not bear it, until after the last fight with his parents when he had slammed the door, marched down to the shipping dock, and secured a job on a barge headed for the new land.

He had landed in Nova Scotia, bought a horse and a small sleigh, and headed west through Canada and then into Vermont. He was on his way to the great waters of Lake Champlain. On the trail he met several old men dressed in their wool jackets and pants carrying fishing poles and red flags attached to wires. They were off to ice fish for the day. "Morning to you, then," John said as he approached them.

"Morning. You're sure a long way from home, young man, where you from?" the fisherman carrying a three-legged milking stool said. "You got a strange accent. Where you headed?"

"I'm from Scotland, and I'm wanting to cross the lake. Is the ice safe?"

"Yup, we've had us one cold winter, but that place over there, the man holding the red flags pointed south, ain't fit for man or beast. That is what they call deer hunting country. Good for hunting and fishing, not living and not nothing this time o' year. Why, I don't even know if you can walk through there now with all the blowdown."

"Blowdown?"

"Yup, we get us some terrible storms up here, and the winds and snow knock trees down on top of each other. Makes for hard walking." None of that deterred John. He was more determined than ever to go to this place where he could live alone off the land and forget the past.

The large man with the red and black checked jacket spoke up, "Well then, young man, if you aren't taking our advice about not going, I'll tell you this, just past the river's edge about one hundred feet into the forest and you'll see a military road that will take you to a port called Rouses Point, but I ain't been on the road in years so it might be grown up. We got to be on our way now." The men wished him luck, turned, and continued walking on a path toward the lake. John thanked them and within ten minutes found himself standing on the Lake Champlain shore with the bitter freezing wind lashing at his face. He could easily see the tree-lined shore on the opposite side of the lake; it was New York State, and it was where she lived.

John cautiously stepped out onto the ice. Fear rose like an icy snake through his veins. If he went through, he would die out here and no one would know. He jumped, and the ice still held so he slowly coaxed his horse, Loch, out onto the ice. He heard a loud crack, which terrified him, but they did not fall through. However, Loch backed off the ice, and it took several minutes for John to persuade him to move forward. Finally, he bent to his master's will and walked onto the snowy lake. It was late afternoon when they reached the border and John took his first step onto American soil.

John knew Jenny was walking on this same New York soil, but he did not want to interfere in her life. His cousin had told him that Jenny and Fergus lived near the St. Lawrence River and had a son, so John decided to go to this uninhabited land to live so he was away from Jenny. He could not bear to see her with another man. Grief had gripped John like a giant jaw when Jenny left. At times, he could not catch his breath, and he cried when he had to venture past the Doddses' farm. After a few years, he tried to go on outings with women, but he kept comparing them to Jenny, so he stopped. Now he would live a hermit's life in this new place.

"Come on, Loch, we've got places to go and food to catch." After crossing the lake, John felt exhilarated. He found the old military path, followed it, and true to what the fishermen told him, he ended up in Rouses Point. John had read about the famous Fort Blunder, built by Americans in Rouses Point in the early 1800s to protect the territory from an attack by British Canada during the War of 1812. Ironically, halfway through construction, they discovered it was being built on Canadian soil, so they had to abandon the fort.

Once in the town, John paid for a room. He would stay here a few days and then head west to a place called Pendleton where he would buy a piece of land with his money from Uncle Walter. While at Oxford, John learned that he could buy land in northeastern New York for next to nothing. The pamphlet he read talked about how fertile the soil was. He dreamed of building a small cabin for shelter and living off the land like Natty Bumppo, the intriguing character in James Fenimore Cooper's novels. John carried *The Pioneer* and *Last of the Mohicans* with him. He had read them several times. Someday he vowed to visit Cooperstown, where Cooper lived most of his life. Also, Cooper's novel, *The Spy* was based on his uncle's novel, *Waverly*, made up of adventures and romances centered in Scotland.

The following week, John loaded his horse and sleigh on a ferry barge that was running on open water from Rouses Point to Port Henry, New York. This section of the lake rarely froze over because a strong current ran through it. By now, John was very low on funds. He had heard that there was an iron mill near this deer hunting country that needed workers. He had heard about this area from an Oxford friend whose grandfather, Abner Belden, had come to the ragged settlement called Pendleton, helped run the first sawmill, and built one of the first log cabins in the settlement.

The ferry let him off in Port Henry, a small settlement hosting ten families. However, when he entered the local store, he heard only

French-speaking men and several Iroquois Indians speaking their native language. Luckily, he had studied French at university and could understand and speak the language well enough to ask for his supplies. One Iroquois offered to guide him to where he wanted to go, but John did not want to spend the money he wanted. The man behind the store counter warned him not to go into those woods around Pendleton alone. "Mister, it is dangerous for the locals, so I fear you will not fare well being a stranger in these parts." John thanked the man, but although John had nearly died from polio, he did not fear the unknown if the unknown was in the woods. He did not fear thieves, as he had nothing to steal except his rifle; however, he did notice an Iroquois staring a little too intently at the weapon. Feeling increasingly uncomfortable, John paid for his room and left. That night as he slept in a cold corner of the cabin that served as hotel, store, and restaurant; he dreamed of walking peacefully through the bare hardwoods and snow-ladened pines. He could hear the cracking sounds of pileated woodpeckers and the soft thud of snow falling from the branches of the large elm trees as the temperature rose in the afternoon sun.

Suddenly, a shot rang out; a scream ripped through the mountain air, and John felt himself falling. He awoke with a start, sat straight up in bed, grabbed his rifle, and cautiously peered out the window. All was well. He had had a nightmare. He grabbed his deerskin pants and jacket, put on his coonskin cap, and headed down to the livery to get his horse. The Frenchman had recommended he sell the sleigh and go on horseback, taking all he could in his saddlebags, which he did.

Harold, the old, curly-haired man at the livery, had taken good care of his horse. "Where you headed, Lad?"

"West into those mountains to a place on the Hudson River called Pendleton."

"Rough territory. You sure you want to go there?"

"I am sure."

"Well, keep that gun handy and any other weapon you got as it is a dangerous journey. If you don't get attacked by panthers, wolves, or bear, you could encounter human enemies."

"Human?"

"Yes, we got some bad men in these parts, so you need to be on your toes. Should take old William Tait with you."

"Who is that?"

"Oh, he's an old hermit lives in these parts. Knows this territory better than any man around."

"How much does he charge?"

"He'll take ya there for food or that hat or whatever you got that he fancies or, of course, coins."

"He will?"

"Sure will, but the only problem is you've got to watch him. He won't hurt you, but he'll take from you if the takin' is good. He's lived alone so long, some folks think he's crazy, but considering where you're going, I'd say he may not be the crazy one." John thought about this for a moment and decided to take this man's advice. "You'll find old William a mile outside of town. Stop just past the big rock and shoot your gun three times and he'll come out to meet you."

"Really, just shoot three times in the air?" John remembered the shot in his dream.

"Yup."

"How will I know which rock?"

"Oh, you'll know; biggest one out there. Got a birch growing out of the side of it. Oh, and just so you know, Pendleton ain't the name no more. It's called Newcomb."

"No, my map says it's Pendleton."

"Old map. A couple of years ago a retired military man who served in that war up here bought it and changed it to his name, Newcomb; believe it was Daniel Newcomb"

They shook hands and John thanked him, half believing what he told him. Soon, John crested a knoll and there on the right side was the biggest rock he had ever seen with a birch tree growing out of the side. He pulled out his rifle and shot three times. Within fifteen minutes, he saw the bushes to the right move. Then a gray mule emerged. Riding the mule was a man with long gray or dirt-white hair and a beard the same color that hung down past the mule's neck. He wore a long bearskin black coat and carried an old sawed-off shotgun at his waist. It was pointed straight at John's head. The man's face was wrinkled and weather beaten, and he wore a fur cap with the fox head pointing straight at John like the gun. "What can I do for ya?" the man asked in a raspy voice.

"Harold at the livery said I might hire you to lead me into the mountains."

"Oh, he did, did he? What ya payin?"

"What do you want?"

The old man chuckled. "I could use a decent fish pole. Mine just broke, and I'll need some fish before I can get another one whittled." John did have a fish pole that William had seen when he was riding toward him.

"Well, I don't know. This is a gift and I don't...."

"Good then," William retorted, turned, and disappeared into the black forest before John had a chance to think. He sat on his horse and thought about it for a moment. How far had William gone? This pole was his Uncle Walter's and he hated to give it up, but having a guide was more important than preserving this fish pole. Uncle Walter would have called him a nincompoop if he hadn't made the trade. He smiled when he thought of his uncle and some of the words he used. He missed him, and he knew Uncle Walter would have loved this country.

"Wait! John shouted, Wait!" He thought he might have to shoot his gun again, but William suddenly materialized from behind the massive white pine to right of him.

"Okay then," William said as he walked over and took the fish pole out of the satchel.

"You were there all along, weren't you? You knew I would change my mind."

"Yup, I didn't go far. No sense walking more than yer feet need to."

"I guess," John replied. "My name is John Scott."

"I am William. Just William." John found out that William hunted in the woods around Newcomb. "Good fishing there too. Big

207

trout in a long lake nearby and big moose. No people but big moose. You'll like it if you make it."

"Okay," John murmured thinking that he really did not want to meet up with a moose, big or small. He would stick to deer. The last remark did not sit well with him either. Why would he not make it? 'How big are the fish?' he thought, as Lock plodded along the snow-covered path. William led for a while then slowed down and let John lead. John continued to think about what was coming and not what was happening. When John came out of his reverie, he discovered that William was no longer with him. He could not believe it. The old man just disappeared without a sound. John shouted for ten minutes, but this time William did not appear. Then John realized that he had been tricked. He should have given him the pole at the end of the trail. Harold had warned him. Now he was on his own. Now he must listen carefully to what people out here told him. He must be alert and ready for anything. He pulled out his compass. He knew Newcomb was west, and he assumed he was on the trail headed there. According to Harold, it was only a day's ride, but over Ragged Mountain; there was no way around it.

The sun shot brilliant rays of yellow on the white snow. In places, John had to shield his eyes, but most of the time the massive fir trees blocked the sunlight. About the time the sun was straight overhead, John stopped and sat on a rotting log. He had packed smoked venison, and he took a gnaw of it then tipped up his canteen to drink, heard a low growl, turned his head, and saw a gray wolf standing a couple feet from him. He looked over at Loch, and there was his rifle sticking out of the side of his saddle. 'How stupid,' he thought. Before that thought ended, the animal lunged, teeth barred, growling incessantly. John had only a moment to pull his knife out; the wolf was on him before he could lift his arm. It went straight for John's neck. John rolled over, hitting it with his fist, and knocking it away just long enough to get the knife up in front of him. Now John was on his back staring straight into the wolf's face as it pounced and trapped him, straddling him with all four legs. This was John's chance. He was staring at the beast's chest. He had to make this good, or this would be the end of him. He drew back the knife and plunged it as hard as he could into the wolf's chest. He heard a piercing scream and then silence as he tried to get out from under the animal. He heard a thud as the wolf fell to the ground, half on John's legs.

John sat on the log for a time contemplating the incident. He gutted it, skinned it, and thought about staying for the night and having wolf for dinner, but he reasoned that where there is one, there is a pack, so he took the pelt, got on his horse, and continued on knowing now always to keep his gun at his side.

It was dark when he rolled into the little settlement perched on the banks of the great Hudson River. He searched until he found a flat space under a giant white pine. He gathered pine boughs for a bed, built a fire, crawled into his sleeping sack, and looked out at the land before him. He could see the outline of mountains in the distance. Tonight, the moon was full. Its light rays bounced off the blue waters of the lake bordered by pines stationed like sentinels around the perimeter. Ah, yes, this was home. He felt it. He heard it in the hoot of the great horned owl and the splash of the fish jumping in the nearby water. He would have fish for breakfast. Before he nodded off, he saw her black hair blowing in the wind as she ran down the path so many years ago.

Chapter XIX

1830

A few miles down the trail from Newcomb in Chestertown, Jeff Rutherford was getting ready to meet a man named Joel Plumley, and it was not to be a good thing. Joel and Sarah Plumley, their son, John, and daughter, Rachel, came from Vermont. Joel moved his family to the farm bordering Jeff's land. Joel seemed to think that his land included the row of maples along the outer east fence line. At least he had set up taps on the holes Jeff had tapped years prior to this one. When Jeff saw what Joel had done, he reasoned that the man did not understand that those maples were on his land. The following morning, Jeff found Joel out in his barn and approached him. "Hey, Joel."

"Yes," Joel replied.

"I see you've tapped those maples down on the fence line."

"Yup, appears so."

"Well, didn't you know that those are my maples?"

"Then why are they on my property?"

"They aren't. They are on mine. I've been tapping them for years."

"Oh, lucky for you the owner before me didn't complain."

Jeff was getting frustrated. "Right, he didn't complain because they weren't his."

Joel straightened up and walked over to Jeff, looked him straight in the eyes and said, "Well, they're mine."

"They are not. They are on my land. I have a survey that says so."

"So do I," Joel retorted, "Now get off my property and leave me alone."

Jeff was furious. He turned and shouted back, "You won't get away with this! I'll be back!" He headed straight for his safe and pulled out his deed. He looked at the plat showing that row of maples were on his land. He grabbed it and marched back over to the Plumleys' where he found Joel out in the field mending a fence. Raising his hand as walked across the field to meet him, Jeff shouted, "Here it is. Proof. Look at this survey. That property is mine."

"I ain't looking at anything you got. Go away."

"Then you'll be looking at it through jail bars if I take it down to the sheriff." That got Joel's attention, so he walked over and let Jeff show him the plat. "See, there it is: that fence line on my land. It is mine."

"So, it be. Guess I was wrong. Okay, then, it's yours."

"Okay, now you need to get your taps out of my trees."

"Uh huh," Joel retorted and went back to his fence. A week later, there was a terrible fire. It started down at the fence line and burned most of the maple trees to the ground. Joel Plumley was the first one at the scene to fight the fire, telling the Rutherfords how sorry he was this had happened. Jeff was seething as he glared at this lunatic neighbor. He had a lucrative syrup business and more maple trees, but these trees had been his best producers. Suddenly, the timeframe for moving to the property he had purchase in Newcomb zoomed forward at an amazing speed.

However, though the two men were at odds with each other, the women had become friends. Celia, Jenny, and Sarah Plumley exchanged recipes and watched each other's children, including baby Julia who was born soon after Jenny arrived. Celia introduced Sarah and Jenny to the rest of the women, including Martha Wheeler, Dan's sister, who was a midwife. After two years in Chestertown, Jenny, Ann, and Ned knew everyone, even though with the new mills going up on the banks of the creeks, Chestertown was a growing community. The post office run by Joel Potter handled mail for many of the settlements north of Chestertown. Because most men were logging, working at the mills, or farming, Joel hired Ann to help him for a few hours a day at the post office even though there was town gossip about sightings of her and Patrick.

True to his word, Patrick and his sister did come to town, and Ann and Patrick were seen together quite often, perhaps too often. Jenny reminded her sister that romance between a white and an Indian was taboo. Ann's response was, "Oh, much like in Scotland between a tenant farmer and royalty." That stopped Jenny in her tracks, though she did try to tell Ann that the consequences could be the same: having to give up the one you love. However, Ann would not let anyone tell her what she could do. Her parents barely could when she was a child so as an adult, she was not about to listen to anyone else. She traveled with the men, hunted with them, visited the Abenaki village, and walked down the middle of Chestertown with Patrick. She and Patrick discussed marriage and living with the tribe, but Ann could not bring herself to leave her sister while she was still grieving Fergus. Besides, Ann was the major hunter for the family. Patrick understood the situation and did not push her to make any decisions. Ann had learned Abenaki quite well, and Patrick had learned more English.

On her first visit back to Patrick's home, Namito greeted her as if he knew she was coming. Ann recalled him saying that they would meet again. He knew, but how? After seeing him many more times, she began to accept that Namito was a healer and a wise old man, and she need not question his abilities.

During one of Patrick's visits, Jeff and Celia announced that they had made the decision to move to Newcomb the following spring. Jeff and Jeff Jr. would go in March to prepare the land along with two of the hired hands on the farm. Celia, Isaac, and Ernie would finish up the maple tapping. Jeff and his oldest son would come back for the sugaring. After the initial shock, Ann, Jenny, and Ned volunteered to help with the farm and the tapping.

"I am so excited for you," Jenny remarked, but underneath she feared their fate once the Rutherfords left. They had their own place now, but Jeff and his son did a lot for her. She was able to plant a garden on their land and tend to several sheep and chickens. They were very generous people.

She remembered how they took care of her when the baby came. Julia came early, only a few months after they arrived. Jenny was weak, as she had just come down with a bad cold. "Oh, my Lord, Celia, it is too early. It can't be. Not now," Jenny cried.

"Well, it is coming, Jenny, whether we like it or not." She looked over at her friend. Her hair was seeped in sweat. She felt her head. She was burning up. "Ann, go get Sarah Plumley, and Ned, you get Martha Wheeler!" Within minutes, both women came running. The four women worked throughout the day and night. On September 10, 1825, at 5:30 in the morning Julia Walton was born. Jeff, Ned, and the rest of the men heard the cries and felt relieved. However, the cries were no insurance of survival. Julia only weighed a little over five pounds, and everyone thought she would not make it. Jenny was not lucid as her fever had spiked, and she was now in a deep sleep. On Patrick's request, Namito had arrived that evening, brought medicine, chanted over the infant and Jenny throughout the night, and the next day, Jenny opened her eyes and asked for her baby. Amazingly, the baby began to suckle right away and appeared to be holding her own.

Within days, Julia began to gain weight and in no time was thriving. They were so grateful to all who helped. A few days later as Jenny watched Celia prepare breakfast for her family, her thoughts turned to this amazing family, the Rutherfords. They had lost most of their wealth but were able to pick up, move on, and begin building wealth again by working hard and creating three successful businesses—the farm, the syrup business, and the beer business. Celia broke through Jenny's reverie.

"I am sorry we couldn't tell you sooner, but we didn't know until yesterday that the farm sold, and we don't want Joel Plumley to know."

"I understand," Jenny replied, "and he will not hear a word from us, right?" she looked at Ann, Patrick, and Ned. They all shook their heads. Jeff and Celia did not want Joel to know they had sold the farm or where they were moving. Later that evening Celia made tea, and she and Jenny sat down at the log table.

"You know, Jenny, you are welcome to go with us. It is wild territory I understand, so we are not sure what to expect, but I hate to leave you here alone."

"I am not alone, Celia. I have friends here, my job, my sister, Ned, and Julia but, Celia, I want to ask you this. How do you do it?"

"Do what?"

"Follow your husband and leave everything behind. Aren't you scared?"

"Of course, I am, but I trust the Lord, and I trust my husband."

"Well, I thought I trusted God, too, but now, I don't know so much. What about the wolves, bears, and panthers out there and the horrible thieves…."

"Oh, I understand your fear, Jenny. Some terrible men killed your husband but look at the men you have met—Namito, Jeff, Patrick, Dan, and so many other good, honest men."

"I know. I guess you are right. I wish I could be more like Ann. She doesn't fear anything."

"Well she is a unique woman, and she also knows how to defend herself. Do you know how to shoot a gun, Jenny?"

"My father taught me years ago, but I don't think I could hit anything now."

"Then, that must change. You need to be able to protect yourself in these mountains." And so began shooting lessons. Jenny's teacher was Ann. She learned to shoot, pull a bow, and throw a knife, not as well as Ann, but well enough to protect herself.

Throughout that year, Jeff, Jeff Jr., and Isaac visited the land they had bought in Newcomb, and on March 8, 1831, as the sun was rising from the morning dew, Jeff and his two sons began the journey through the thick forest to begin planting and building on the Rutherford's new land. They arrived as the sun was setting behind the distant mountains. Newcomb had a sawmill, a gristmill, a general store, blacksmith shop, and several cabins along the water. They unloaded supplies on their fifty acres along the water's edge and the next day began cutting down trees and building a lean-to to sleep in and house their tools. First, they focused on plowing and getting the seed in and then on building the cabin. There were few women in the town except for Sarah Dornburgh, who had three children and was seen out in the fields helping her husband, John. The Chandler brothers' wives were seen about town and were rumored to make the best pickles and jelly around.

In June, Jeff returned to Chestertown to bring the family to their new cabin. By this time, Celia was showing as their baby was due in September. She wanted Jenny to come and help her when the baby came. Jenny had discussed with Ann and Ned the possibility of going with the Rutherfords. Ann was excited about going, but Ned and Julia, who had close school friends, did not want to go. It did not help that Ned remembered what had happened to his father on the last trip. Patrick took him aside and told him about the great hunting grounds. "Ned, I will teach you how to track and shoot the bow and arrow." Patrick also assured Ned that his Aunt Ann and he had made sure those bad men would never hurt anyone again.

Ned recalled a couple of weeks last fall when Ann had been away. She had told the family that she and Patrick were going to Rossie to see Helen and Thomas. Ann, Patrick, and Gizos had actually sailed across Lake Champlain to find the men who had tortured Ann's family. Pretending to be a patron wanting to purchase a ticket, Ann found out the name of the captain of the boat that was still running on the lake. His name was a Captain LaRue, and he had had the same crew for years.

One night when the crew was returning from a run after all the passengers had left and the sailors were readying the boat for the next run, Ann, Patrick, and Gizos boarded the boat carrying guns and knives. They captured the crew, dragged them into the forest, and let them watch their boat burn. Ann told them that they had come to pay them back for what they had so 'generously given them.'

"What? Why? I never did anything to you. Why are you doing this?" Captain LaRue lamented in perfect English as he stared at the flames shooting up into the sky.

'You don't remember me? Of course,' Ann thought, 'I am sure I am only one of the many you have robbed and hurt. Well, you will remember me now, won't you?' Ann made them listen to what they had done to her family.

"No, please, it wasn't us," whined the red-faced, big-lipped captain, but his two crewmen started blaming him saying that they had had to follow orders or the captain would kill them.

"Well, because you followed orders, you killed a man I loved. You killed my sister's husband. You threw him overboard like fish guts and left us to die in a little boat on this huge river!" Ann shouted, as Patrick and Gizos loaded the men onto the boat they had rented in Port Henry. When Ann told them where they were going, two of the men cried, and Captain LaRue began to plead for his life, telling them that he had children and grandchildren. They took the men to Patrick and Gizos' Abenaki camp where they were kept in confinement for months. When the tribe released the scared, hungry men, they warned them to go back to Canada and never set foot on United States soil again and that if they did, the Iroquois, Algonquin, and Mohawk would know and would take care of them. The men scurried off in the same clothes they came with never to be seen again in those parts. Ann returned home, and when she wrote to her brother, Robert, she told him, but Thomas, Helen, and Jenny never knew what she had done.

Meanwhile, Jenny was feeling increasingly concerned about being separated from her best friend, Celia, and not being there to help with the birth of her baby. Though Ned and Julia didn't want to leave, they didn't want their best friends, the Rutherfords, to leave either.

The turning point for Jenny was the arrival of Uncle Wright and his cousin, John Huntley. Aunt Catherine had received a letter from Jenny telling her that the Rutherfords were moving to Newcomb, New York. The decision to move was not difficult for Aunt Catherine and Uncle Wright. They felt it would be safer for Jenny and the children to go with the Rutherfords, so she sent Wright and John up to convince Jenny to go.

After hearing what they had to say and knowing that they would accompany her to this new place, Jenny agreed to go. The plan was that once they arrived in Newcomb, Uncle Wright would stay awhile and then return to Rossie. John Huntley would stay with Jenny and the children. He was a trapper and guide, and had been to Newcomb several times.

Her only prospect for a husband in Chestertown had been a widower who had a small farm. He wanted to court her and take care of her, but Jenny could not make a place in heart for him as wonderful and secure as that sounded. Here she was going off to another strange place at the mercy of friends again.

On June 10, 1830, they loaded up the wagons and began the haul through the woods to this new place on the great river, and as soon as Jenny saw the rushing waters of the Hudson, her thoughts raced to the River Tweed and John Scott.

Chapter XX

1834

John Scott lived in the woods in his cabin next to the Hudson River. His hair grew down past his shoulders, and his beard reached to his belt. He would soon need to cut it off, a thing he did once a year. His camp was a small cabin, several lean-tos where he hung meat and kept his tools, and an outhouse. Inside the rough cabin was a fireplace, an old iron woodstove, and a small bunk with a bearskin blanket and a fleece-filled pillow. He had built a log table and shelves that held bullets, a few knives, a gun, and all the books written by his uncle. Throughout his travels, he carried those books with him, and he read them sitting by the fire on cold, wintry nights. Folks in town knew him as John the hermit. He spoke very little and only ventured into town to get supplies. He worked a little on cutting a road from Newcomb to Chestertown with a man named St. John who owned the local sawmill. They named it Cedar Point Road, and while doing this work he met a man named Plumley. He had seen him come through town a couple of times, but had no idea that this man knew Jenny. One day while in town at Bissell's Store, he ran into an old teacher, James Dodds, who amazingly recognized John after all these years.

"Well, well, John Scott, fancy meeting you here," James said, walking up to him and putting his hand out.

John recognized him, shook his hand, and inquired, "Mr. Dodds, I never thought I would see you in these parts. What are you doing here?"

"Well, I might ask the same question, but I will tell you that I was assigned a teaching position with a wealthy family, the Whitneys. I'm here to price log cutting for a camp they want to build."

"Sir, I never thought you would leave Scotland. I thought you wanted nothing to do with the colonies" John remembered James' reputation as a story teller, so he did not really believe he was working for a wealthy family.

"Ah, people change, son; people change, as I can see you have." He scanned John from head to foot. "Why are you here and dressed like that? Aren't you a lawyer?"

John had to tell him he was not; not wanting to talk long, he asked, "So what about your kin; how are the Doddses?"

"Oh, well, I guess okay; except the oldest girl had a run-in with her parents and left home."

"Really? You mean she didn't come to America with them?"

"No, stayed in Scotland," James' keen eyes noticed the catch in John's breath.

"Well, James, isn't it strange that I got letters from her when she was on a ship headed this way. You think she got the captain to turn around and take her back?" John could not believe this man was part of such strong, proud family. "Well, I have to go. Good luck with that

222

wealthy family." Before James could say anything else, John was halfway down the street. James Dodds was an anomaly in the family. He could not make it in Scotland, so perhaps he could survive here among fewer people. However, John wondered what would happen to him once he used his sharp tongue on one of these tough woodsmen.

A couple of weeks earlier, as John was cooking breakfast at his camp, a man came by. John invited him in and shared coffee and breakfast with him. The man's name was Ebenezer Emmons and he was hired to survey and name the mountains in this area The name he had chosen was 'Adirondack Mountains.'

"What?" John asked.

"Adirondack," Emmons repeated. He related that Adirondack was the Anglican version of the Mohawk word, 'Ratirontaks,' meaning bark eater. Sitting around the campfire that night, Emmons told John that the Mohawk tribe called the Algonquins bark eaters because the Algonquins ate the buds and bark off trees when food was scarce. Emmons thanked John for his hospitality and left the next morning. They would meet several more times before the surveyor finished the job and returned to his home.

In the meantime, Jenny was working on a place of her own. On a chilly spring morning, she was driving the wagon to the St. John's sawmill in Newcomb when she saw a man dressed in tattered clothes, deerskin boots and jacket, and a fur hat that covered his head and most of his face. 'Hmm, I guess that is John the hermit,' she thought as she drove on to the sawmill. Today she was getting logs cut for the cabin they were building on a piece of land she was buying from Jeff. She had been here two years and had learned how to hunt, fish, and trap just like Ann.

Ann and Patrick did eventually marry in a little ceremony in Newcomb with family, friends, and their son. A traveling minister, Reverend Todd, married them. It did not seem to matter to the people here that Patrick was Abenaki and Ann white. It was a tough life up here, and most people did not have time for such matters, which was a good thing because Patrick and Ann's son, Joseph, was now five years old. To anyone other than Ann, this matter of having a child out of wedlock would have been a disaster, but Ann was proud of her little boy and paid no attention to any wagging tongues.

Patrick, Ann, and Jenny were building the cabin together. The cabin would have a loft for the children and two separate bedrooms for the adults. Ned, who was a teenager now, spent many summer nights outside in the lean-to they had built before they put up the cabin.

Though Jenny had not been able to attend her sister Mary's wedding all those years ago, the two women exchanged letters, and soon after Jenny and Ann arrived in Newcomb, Thomas, Helen, Robert, George, Mary, and her husband made the journey up from Rossie. Of course, George, now being nineteen, wanted to stay; however, the family farm in Rossie needed tending, so he returned but vowed to come back someday. His brother Tom had found his true love, Henriette. They were married and living on land near the St. Lawrence River in Waddington, New York. They were watching his father's farm while Thomas and Helen were visiting their children and grandchildren in Newcomb. One afternoon, Thomas wandered out to the lean-to and found Ned writing on a piece of birch bark. "What are you doing there, Lad?"

"Oh, Grandpa, I'm just writing."

"Writing, huh, writing what?"

"This. Do you want to see? It's a poem, but it is not finished."

"Sure." Ned handed him the birch bark, and Thomas read:

In the Adirondacks at breaking sun

I enter the forest with my gun,

scouring the woods for bear or deer,

until the sun shall disappear.

Thomas was amazed that this young boy could write so well. "Where did you learn this, Ned?"

"Oh, my mom has a book written by a Sir Walter Scott, and he wrote a poem about the woods he loved in Scotland. I love my woods, so I wanted to write about my woods and hunting, but it's not finished."

"I see," Thomas said. "Well that fellow, Sir Walter Scott, was quite famous, you know."

"Oh, yes, Grandpa, Ma told me all about him."

"I bet she did. I bet she did, and I wonder when she is going to tell the rest of us."

"What, Grandpa?"

"Oh, nothing, Ned; you keep up the writing. It is very good." Thomas walked back to the cabin debating whether to bring up his suspicions.

He decided that it was Jenny's business, but he hoped that one day she would tell Ned that his great uncle was none other than Sir Walter Scott. On the way home, Helen and Thomas discussed the events that had brought their children to this wooded land. "Well, Thomas, we did raise them to be the best that they could be."

"We did, Lass, that we did, and they are."

"Yes, they are, though I do worry about the horrific winters and the animals they must contend with here in these mountains."

"Have you seen Ann and Jenny shoot?" George asked.

"Yes, Ann, but not Jenny. Does Jenny shoot now?"

"Oh, yes, and she is very accurate. You taught us well, Da."

'As cousin James taught me,' he thought. He had not spoken to James in years. As a boy, Thomas had looked up to James, though he was only a few years older. When James was fifteen, his mother had drowned in the river next to their house. There was a rumor that she had committed suicide, but James' father swore she did not. James' father did well and sent James off to school where he became a teacher. His father was extremely religious and rigid, and some of that rigidity rubbed off on James. When Thomas found out that James had turned Uncle Wright in as a horse thief to get the reward money, Thomas stopped talking to him.

"Thomas?" Helen brought him out of his reflections, reminding Thomas of that night so long ago when they saw that black bear outside of Uncle Wright's house. They laughed as they rode along on the stage, soon entering the vast fields Thomas Dodds had accumulated in fifteen short years. Tomorrow he and Mary would play their pipes before Sunday's church service.

Back in Newcomb, John Scott walked into town; as he was passing the blacksmith shop, he heard the rumble of an oxen wagon. He looked up and saw a woman driving a team of oxen toward the sawmill. He saw her black hair flying in the wind, and it reminded him of Jenny. He lumbered into the trading post with his new pelts and traded them for flour and sugar. He wanted Elisha Bissell to repair his shoes, but he needed more pelts to pay for the work. As Elisha put John's dried goods on the counter, they both heard a woman scream. It was coming a short distance from where John had last seen the wagon. He ran out the door toward the sound. As he peeled around the corner, he saw the wagon. One of the oxen was down, and the wagon was tipped on its side. 'Oh, Lord,' thought John, 'what is going on?' He saw a black flash against the bright sun, pulled out his rifle, and shot at a black panther that had jumped on the back of one of the oxen. The panther screamed and fell back. He hurried to the wagon and looked at the seat where the woman had been. She was gone! He feared the worst. Maybe she was under the wagon. The downed ox was bellowing, and John ran to it. It had scratches on its side but appeared to be okay. It could not stand as it was still attached to the wagon that was on its side. "Lass, Lass, where are you?" John yelled searching frantically for the woman. Three of the Chandler brothers came running out of the livery and righted the oxen and wagon. The woman was not under the wagon, so they began looking around for her.

"Over here. She's over here!" John and the brothers saw Daniel and Polly Bissell motioning to them. Polly was kneeling cradling the woman's head. She was not moving. When he reached them, he saw strands of black hair splashed all around her like a halo. Her tiny face was as white as the paint on the livery.

"Is she okay?" he asked breathlessly.

"Yup, think so," Polly replied. "She's coming around now." John Dornburgh and a few others had gathered around. The Dornburghs had only been in Newcomb about six months. John Scott walked over and knelt beside the woman. He could not believe what he was seeing. "No, it can't be." He moved her hair away from the side of her face as she groaned and opened her eyes. She stared, transfixed. "My God, that face. It looked like John Scott, but it can't be."

"Am, am I dead?"

"No, ma'am," replied Sarah Dornburgh, "you are alive." By this time, several of the Keller women had arrived with medicine, along with Captain Peter Sabattis, who had just come up from the lake.

"But...."

John came out of his stupor. It was Jenny! "Jenny, don't talk."

"John?"

"Yes."

"Are we in heaven?" She reached up and touched his hair, still blond with bits of gray. She stared into his sky-blue eyes. "Oh, Lord have mercy, it is you; it is you, John Scott."

"'tis, indeed and, no, we are not in heaven."

"You two know each other?" John Dornburgh asked, as Jenny began to push herself off the ground.

"Yes, from the old country; Scotland," John the hermit replied. "Now, Jenny, you be careful. Here let me help you." He put his arm around her and helped her to her feet. She felt a little dizzy but leaned into John's strong arm. They looked deeply into each other's eyes, and before they knew what was happening, they were in each other's arms hugging. Jenny was crying loudly, tears streaming down her face.

"John! Oh, my God, John." As soon as his arms were around her, she buried her face in his neck and smelled the familiar scent she had cried for night after night alone in her bed. They both forgot about the people around them. Once the Bissells knew Jenny was okay, they quietly disappeared, motioning for the rest of the people to let the lovers bask in their glorious reunion.

John helped her up, and they walked over to the town well and sat down. "God, John, where were you all these years? I wrote."

"I know, but I missed you so much I could not write back. I had to disappear."

"So, you came here. Where do you live?"

"You wouldn't want to know, Jen. I've changed."

She touched his hair. "Yes, I can see that." She wanted to ask him so many questions like why he was here. 'What work would a

229

lawyer have out in this wilderness,' she wondered? She did not ask any questions because living in the wilderness had taught her not to question. Men came to these parts to escape from many things. Freedom was sacred in these mountains, as sacred as a priest's vow, so men and women in the Adirondacks could carry their secrets safe and hidden.

"Why isn't Fergus driving that wagon, and by the way, you drive it like a man."

"I also shoot like a man, hunt like a man, and live like a man, and so does Ann."

"Well, I would expect it of Ann, but not you."

"I had to adapt."

"Why?"

"John, Fergus was killed several years ago when we were coming from Rossie, New York, to this place."

"Oh Lord, Lass, I am so sorry. I did not know." He touched her arm. After coming to his senses, he did not want to hug her because he knew he smelled bad. He had not had a bath in at least a month. "Children, do you have children?"

"Yes, John. I have two: Ned is fifteen, and Julia is five."

"Ned, huh?"

"Well his first name is Elmer and middle name Ned, but we call him Ned. How is Uncle Walter?"

"He died two years ago. I went back for his funeral."

"Oh, I am so sorry to hear that. He was a unique, wonderful man. And your family, are they well?" John did not want to talk about

230

his family. He told her that they had disowned him and that he had left Oxford early.

"Yes, Uncle Walter was a unique man. Thank you," John replied.

"I can't believe you left Oxford. My God, I can't believe you are here. I am sorry you are separated from your family." Suddenly she remembered why she had come to town. " Lord, it is getting late. John, I need to get this lumber back to Jeff."

"Jeff Rutherford?"

"Yes."

"Oh, is that where you are staying? I've seen him around, but I don't say much."

"Yes, I have a small cabin on his property and live with my cousin, John, and my Uncle Wright."

"Wright Rule?"

"Yes, the horse thief; I know, but that is just a story. He is a trapper; maybe the best around, but he is on his way back to Rossie right now."

John wanted to go with her and help her but was ashamed of the way he looked and smelled. "Jenny, I live in the woods. I bathe in the river, and I trap and sell pelts for my supplies. I must leave now before you get sick from my smell." He backed away.

Jenny did not know what to think. She had waited so long for this moment, and now that it was here, confusion reigned in her head. This certainly did not look like the man she had been dreaming about for years. When she hugged him, he felt the same, but there was

Gail Huntley

something different about him. He seemed distant, not the warm, gentle boy she had left so many years ago. "John, you must come to dinner."

"No, Jen, I am so glad to see you, but I can't. I am not the man you knew."

"And I am not the girl you knew. We all change," Jenny replied, though she agreed that he had changed drastically. "I must go, John. Please come for supper tomorrow night. We will have it at the Rutherfords. Come at 5:00."

"I'll try. Good to see you again, Jenny." By this time Ann and Patrick had heard about the accident. They arrived just as John was walking back through the store door. They made Jenny sit while they loaded the wagon and took it to the Rutherfords. Afterwards, Jenny rushed home and told the Rutherfords about John and her accident. Celia made her lie down. "Jenny, I can't believe that hermit out there is John Scott."

"Me neither," replied Jeff. They were shocked that he was the hermit. They had seen him in broad daylight and not recognized him. Of course, Jeff had barely known him in Lessudden, but he had met him and knew of him. "Well, I am glad he is coming to supper. It will be good to talk about the old country. You said he went back to Scotland two years ago."

"Yes," Jenny said, thinking that all this time he was close to her and she did not know, and when 5:00 the next night came, John Scott did not. Instead, he sat staring at the campfire wishing he had never seen her. That night, he cried like he had cried when he was a boy. He
232

cried for her, for what he had become, for his Uncle Walter, and for Fergus because he had been good to Jenny. Mostly, he cried for all the memories of kisses on the banks of the Tweed, sweet caresses at SandyKnowe, and holding her hand along the lane. These were moments that could never be replaced, love that would never be fulfilled. He vowed that he would finish his traplines in the morning, sell them at the trading post, and move deeper west to the place with the long lake. He knew this lake was abundant with fish, and the surrounding woods full of game. He could not face Jenny again knowing he could not have her, not because she was a peasant and he was royalty, but because he was a peasant and she was royalty.

Gail Huntley

Chapter XXI

On a clear day in May, Jeff Rutherford walked out of the gristmill and bumped into a man who was rushing up the steps.

"Watch where you're going mister," the man bellowed. That voice! No, it couldn't be. Jeff stopped, looked to his right, and stared straight into the black eyes of Joel Plumley.

"Me?" Jeff fumed; "you're the one who came rushing up the steps not looking where you're going." Then Jeff noticed the other men with Joel. St. John owned the sawmill, and he had met the other two a couple times: James McCarthy from the old country and Colonel Sage, a war hero from the French and Indian Wars.

The Colonel interrupted the two men, "Morning Jeff."

"Morning, Colonel. Where you men headed?"

"West to the long lake."

"Oh, I been up that way. Looked at some land over there."

"Yup, cheap, dirt cheap. You interested?" St. John asked.

"Hell, no. He ain't interested," Joel sputtered.

Jeff looked at the dark-eyed, raven-haired man for a moment and without thinking said, "Sure, I'm interested. See me when you get back." He looked straight at Joel, whose face was beet red in anger.

"Well, don't even think of getting anything near me."

"Of course, I wouldn't. I don't like fires."

"Why you!" Joel stood within inches of Jeff.

In the meantime, St. John and Sage continued up the steps toward the sawmill, "Get over here, Plumley," Colonel ordered; "we don't have time for this. We got to get on that trail if you want to get home anytime soon."

"Home? Thought no one was living out there," John said.

"No one is except me and my family." Joel piped up.

"And Dave Keller," interjected St John.

"Oh, the one with all the girls living here in town?" Jeff asked.

"Yup. He and that young guy, Abram Rice, are preparing the land and going to send for the wife and kids next year," St. John replied; Jeff turned around, and they walked through the door of the grist mill together, leaving Joel trailing behind.

Jeff had been on that trail to the long lake but had not gone all the way to the lake. Patrick had some friends from the tribe who hunted there, so the next day, Patrick took Jeff with him on the trail to the lake. They walked a military road that took them to the foot of the lake. Jeff stood on the sandy beach next to the outlet of this beautiful lake and looked south. The water was bluer than any water he had ever seen. The trees jammed up against each other and reflected themselves in the clear water. He turned, looked north, and saw ridge after ridge of mountain range that extended as far as the eye could see. To his left he saw two Indians coming out of the thick pine forest. These were Patrick's friends and soon they were standing in front of them. The

236

older one wore deerskin from head to foot and the boy, Mitchell, a brown brimmed hat, a wool jacket, deerskin pants and boots. They both carried a knife on their side and a bow in their hands. Patrick greeted them and then introduced Jeff. "Jeff Rutherford, this is Peter Sabattis and his son, Mitchell."

"Hello," Jeff reached out to shake their hands, but they stood stock still.

Finally, Peter spoke, "Patrick, you want to see land over there." They were facing south, and Peter pointed southwest.

"Yes," Patrick replied. "A man named David Smith told me about some land on a lake."

"Ok, we go this way." Jeff began to follow Peter, Mitchell, and Patrick but these men walked so fast Jeff could not keep up. Soon he was way behind, lost, and the afternoon sun was waning. Jeff had not seen the other men for hours. He looked around, but all he could see were green branches and giant tree trunks. He yelled several times, but there was no reply. He could not believe that they had left him alone in this strange territory, especially Patrick. As he walked, several times he heard a bear grunt. He knew it was following him. Now he stopped to rest, drink some water, and climb a tree to see if he could see the other men. He picked a tall white pine and climbed to the top. As he looked to the southwest, barely two hundred feet away he saw smoke on the edge of a large body of water.

"What are you doing up there?" Patrick said, as he stood beneath the tree.

"What? God, you scared me, Patrick. I didn't hear you coming. What am I doing here? How could you leave me out here in unfamiliar territory by myself?"

"You were not by yourself," Peter said, as he appeared from the woods.

"Sure as hell was."

"No, we were tracking a bear. We were here the whole time, and the bear is over there." Jeff looked, but he could not see a thing. Peter pulled his bow off his shoulder, rested an arrow on the wood, and disappeared into the woods with his grandson. Within a few minutes, they returned dragging a bear. "Supper tonight," Peter said. They spent the night on the edge of a beautiful lake surrounded by green mountains. Jeff fell in love with the place.

"But it is not good for farming, I think," Peter said. "I was going to show you land on the long lake."

"I like this land. I don't care. Do you know who owns it?"

"The animals who live here," replied young Mitchell. "They own it." Jeff decided to find out who owned it. He would talk to the man named Smith who the Indians said lived a short distance away. Before he left, Jeff marked the land and vowed to claim it if no one else had. It was in the wilderness, but if it was cheap or he could homestead it, it would be his.

On their way back, they crossed paths with the hermit coming west on the trail. Jeff acknowledged him and then stopped in his tracks. "John, John Scott, is that you?" The man continued to walk without turning around. Jeff ran back, stood in front of him and said, "John, I know it is you. Jenny told me; where are you going?"

"Hello, Jeff. Yes, it is I, and I am going to settle on the long lake," John replied.

"For God's sake, does Jenny know you are leaving Newcomb?"

"No."

"John, you have to go to her."

"Jeff, don't; you don't know."

"You're going to live in the woods on the long lake now?" Peter asked. He had met John many times hunting in these woods. They had eaten fish together and had many conversations during hunting time. "Better fishing here but very hard winter, very hard land."

"I know."

"He is hiding. This is good hiding place," Peter retorted.

"Hiding, hiding from what?" Jeff questioned.

"From love," Peter replied.

"But she is here now, John. She is only miles away. Why would you leave her again?"

"I have nothing to offer. Look at me, Jeff. I have been living in the woods too long."

"But a good woman can make many hurts go away, John," Peter added. John thought about that for a moment, his heart throbbing as he recalled many years ago hearing her voice at the manor door, seeing her white dress as she came around the path, and smelling her skin when he held her. That smell just a few days ago had taken him back, and he had forgotten for a moment what he had become. But when he

239

moved away, and the scent of Jenny was gone, the reality hit him even harder, and now he was here.

"John, you need to come back. You need to try." Jeff wanted to tell him about Ned. Jenny had told his wife, and his wife, though sworn to secrecy, had told him. "Did you meet the boy, Ned? Did you see him?"

"No, she told me about him and her daughter."

"John, I would like you to come back with Patrick and me. I want to show you something."

"No, I'm packed and headed out."

"Right, John, all packed with your pair of pants, and a shirt and everything you own in that backpack."

"That's right. That is why I can't go back. That is everything I have, so I have nothing to give her."

"Oh, you have much more to give her, trust me." Finally, Jeff, being the persuader that he was, convinced John to go back. They said goodbye to Captain Sabattis and Mitchell and began walking the trail back to Newcomb. Patrick was baffled by what he had witnessed; he was silent on the way back and left the two of them at the outlet of the long lake, so he could fish for a while. When Jeff and John emerged from the fourteen-mile path and crossed the lake, Jeff led John down toward Jenny's cabin.

John kept telling Jeff, "No, I am not going there. I know this is where she lives."

"It's okay, John, she is over at Christine Keller's helping her with canning all week. I want you to meet someone else. Come, we'll

240

wait here." Jeff motioned for John to join him on the porch bench. After waiting about fifteen minutes, they saw a boy coming down the hill. As John watched the boy saunter toward him carrying books, he saw something familiar about him. What was it? It was something in how he carried himself, something about the way he walked.

"Uncle Jeff, hey, what are you doing here? Ma is at the Kellers'."

"Oh, I know. I just wanted you to meet my friend, here."

"Oh, the hermit."

"His name is John, Ned."

"Hi, Ned,"

"Hi, Mister John."

"Just John is fine."

"John used to be your mom's neighbor in Scotland," Jeff said.

"Oh."

"You ever heard of Sir Walter Scott?"

"Sure, I love his writing. We're reading him in school, and Ma brought this book all the way from Scotland." He held out one of the books. It had a picture of Sir Walter on the cover. John knew the book. He had given it to Jenny. "My teacher said I look like him."

'He does look a little like Uncle Walter,' thought John, 'the same long nose, the blond hair, the quirk of a smile always budding at his lips. Oh, and that is who he walks like.'

"Well, got to get my chores done. Nice meeting you, mister. Wish I could live in the woods and have no school or chores to do," he said over his shoulder as he ran toward the cabin.

"Remind you of anybody?" Jeff said, looking John square in the face.

"Uh, my uncle. Strange, he walks like Uncle Walter."

"Strange, huh? Well, how about you think on that awhile. Go back to your camp. It's too late to go back to the long lake, anyway."

"Yes, I guess it is," John said, as he looked up at the setting sun. "Okay, Jeff, I'll stay another night. See you soon."

"Yup," Jeff replied and turned, heading home, hoping John could see what he saw.

John went back to his camp, made a pot of coffee, and looked out into the moonless starry night. When he finished, he rolled out his bedding, crawled in, and fell asleep. Suddenly in the middle of the night, he sat straight up! 'Fifteen years old, blond wavy hair, blue eyes, long nose. Oh, my Lord; could it be? Is it possible that Ned is my son? He has to be. It could not be a coincidence.' As much as he wanted to go right over and confront Jenny, he could not. He questioned his conclusion. 'No, he can't be mine, and if he is, why didn't she write and tell me? Did she know before she left Scotland? If she did, did she choose Fergus over me? Why not? We could not be together at that time in Scotland.' John slept less than two hours. He was up at daybreak on his way to see the woman who could be the mother of his child.

Jenny awoke to a loud noise. She grabbed her gun and crept toward the door. She shouted through the thick log door, "Who goes there?"

"It's me, Jen, John." She put the rifle down and lifted the latch. There stood John looking worse than ever. His eyes were beet red, and his hair stuck out under the hood he wore. "What? What are you doing here?"

"I'm sorry. I know it must be very early or very late, but I had to see you."

She opened the door wider, "Okay, come in. Please, sit down."

"Nope, I can't sit down. I'll get right to it, Jenny. Is Ned my son?"

"What?" Jenny's mouth flew open, and her hand covered her mouth. This is what she had always dreaded, except she thought she would be telling Ned, not John.

"Is Ned mine? I saw him, Jen. I talked to him. He looks like me. He has the cleft in his chin like Uncle Walter, my da, and me, and he walks like Uncle Walter. I know it is crazy and probably not true, but I must know. He is the right age. Just tell me I'm crazy, and I will leave and never bother you again."

Jenny sank down onto the wooden chair. She took a deep breath. Her bottom lip quivered, and her shoulders dropped in resignation. It was time. She had to tell him. Her voice shook as she stammered, "No, John, you are not crazy. Ned is your son." The tears came streaming in torrents down her cheeks.

John could not move or speak. Finally, he said, "Oh my God, I have a son. I have a son! Jenny, why didn't you tell me?"

"Because when I left Scotland I did not know I was pregnant, and by the time I knew we were in Rossie. Fergus offered to marry me.

He loved me and knew the feelings were not equal, but he saved my reputation. I would have been shunned and labeled a whore, and I could not do that to Ned or my family or myself. I knew you were at Oxford, and we would never be able to marry. Ned needed a father, so I married Fergus, and he was a wonderful father to Ned."

"Does Ned know?"

"No."

"Are you ever going to tell him?"

"Yes, I was planning to at the right time."

"And when will that be?"

"Well, John, by the looks of things, it will be now. We will tell him when he wakes up. Is that what you want?"

"Uh, I want him to know he is a Scott, but the timing is up to you, Jen. Oh my God, Jen, it must have been so horrible for you. I am so sorry. I wish I had been there. I should have stayed in school and gotten my papers."

"John, you don't need to worry about that. We are okay. You did what you needed to do." She got up and put her arms around him. The passion shot through her whole being just as it had so many years ago whenever she touched him.

John looked down at her. "Jen, I am sorry I didn't come to dinner that night. I do still love you, but I am not good enough for you. Don't touch me." He pulled her arms down.

Jenny backed away, stared him straight in the eyes, put her hands on her hips, and said, "John Scott, you say you love me. Well, I love you too, and I would hope that if I only had one dress, and I fell on tough times that you would not cringe. Now, I lost you once long ago, and I will not lose you again." She moved toward him and kissed him squarely on the mouth.

"Ma! What are you doing?" Ned said as he peeked over the loft.

"Ned! Come on down here and let me fix your breakfast, and then we have something to tell you," Jenny said.

"But...."

Slowly recovering from that magnificent kiss, John watched the boy climb down the ladder. "Ned, please sit down." And so, it was on this fine morning that Ned Walton learned who he was. He was not happy that Fergus was not his real father, but he knew that Fergus had loved him as a son, and in time he reluctantly accepted that this crazy looking, wild haired man was his real father. However, most of all, he was thrilled to learn that Sir Walter Scott was his uncle.

The next morning while it was still dark, Jeff Rutherford woke to pounding on his door. He stumbled to the door wondering who it could be at this hour. There was John Scott. "My Lord, you are an early riser; sun ain't even peeking out yet."

"No, it isn't, but I got something that can't wait. I need a bath, a shave, and a haircut. Jenny and I are getting married Sunday when the preacher comes."

"What? Jeff shook his head, "wow, guess you figured it all out. Okay; that's good, John, but you think you need it done now at four in the morning?"

By now, Celia was up carrying baby Elizabeth in her arms. "Why, that's the best news I've heard in years. Sure, I can cut your hair and give you a shave, and you can take a bath in our tub."

"Now Celia, I don't know about a...."

"Jeff, hush. We're not doing anything to upset this turnip cart. This is a miracle, and we're going to be a part of it. Miracles are always at strange times, in unplanned places, affecting unprepared people. That's why they're miracles. She woke Sadie up and told her to watch Elizabeth. Ok, let's get started then." She already knew about the event. Jenny had come racing over right after John left the morning before and told Celia. So, that morning John took a real bath, and Celia cut his hair and beard. "Oh, my Lord," Jeff said, "you look just like yourself, John Scott, just like the John we knew back home." On a hill facing the vast range of mountains, Helen, Thomas, all the children and friends witnessed the marriage of John and Jenny Scott.

That fall, the Rutherfords left Newcomb for the land Jeff had seen with Peter Sabattis. Jeff chose a site on a quiet pond. They named it Clear Pond because the water was so transparent. they could see fish swimming in the reflections of the low rolling mountains wrapped in autumn colors. The following spring the Scotts followed, settling on the west bank of Long Lake.

Through the years, once a month, Jeff traveled to town and joined Joel Plumley, David Keller, William Kellogg, Abram Rice, James Sargent, David Smith, William Austin, Francis Smith, Lyman Mix, Lysander Hall, Amos Hough, Isaac Robinson, George Shaw, Peter Van Valkenburg, John Dornburgh, and Thomas Cary at the town meeting. Try as he might to get John to come to the meetings, he could not. Though John no longer lived as a hermit, he remained more comfortable in the quiet of his home with his family.

On dark wintry nights, Jenny Scott would crawl into bed beside her husband, warmed by his nearness. She would remember when she bore the burdens of leaving her country and her love, the horrendous voyage across the ocean, and the death of Fergus. Although these were heartbreaking experiences, they brought her to this spot right now where her loved ones were tucked in their beds in this cozy cabin in the woods. Before closing her eyes, she prayed for her family in Rossie. They had come a long way to find this land. They all had their reasons for being here among the wild creatures of the forest. They all fell in love with this land from the great St. Lawrence River to the highest mountain in the Adirondacks. They were here to stay, and so it all began.

Gail Huntley

BIBLIOGRAPHY

Albert, T. and King, S. (1965) *The History of Hamilton County*. Lake Pleasant, New York: Wilderness Books.

Alchin, W. *Willie Alchin Remembers: St Boswell Fair*. Retrieved January 26, 2017. http://www.stboswells.bordernet.co.uk/history/boswells-fair.html.

Auclair, H. (2000) *French-Canadian Lineage of Emily Bertha Disotell*. Unpublished manuscript.

Benedict, D. & Roy C. (2009, June 7) Abenaki People in the Adirondacks. *Adirondack Journal*. Blue Mountain, NY: Blue Mountain Museum

Bufo, A. (1973, Fall) Workhorse of the Woods. *Adirondack Life*. 20-24.

Cedar Point Road Map. (2017) From the archives of the Newcomb, New York, Historical Museum.

Charles Dalzell & Annie Dodd. (1877) Certified copy of marriage certificate. Waddington, New York.

Dalzell, G. (1937) *Immigration of the Dodds Family to America*. Canton New York.

Donaldson, A. (1921) *History of the Adirondacks* (Book 1). New York: The Century Co.

Eildon Hills Melrose, Scottish Borders UK. (2016). Retrieved December 2016. http://www.touristnetuk.com/scotland/borders.

Emerson, L. (1840-1928). Early Life at Long Lake. Long Lake, New York. Lavonia Stanton Emerson.

Fennessy, L (1996). History of Newcomb. Newcomb, NY: Lana Fennesy

Fenton, A. (1992) *The Island Black House.* Edinburgh, Scotland: HMSO Publications.

Huntley, G. (2013) *Conquering the Wild.* Morgan Hill, CA: Bookstand Publishing.

Huntley, G. (2015) *Long Lake, Adirondack Heartland.* Morgan Hill, CA: Bookstand Publishing.

Huntley, V. (1978) *John Huntley of Lyme Connecticut.* Moodus, CT: Moodus Printing.

John Rule & Mary Dodds (1882) Certified copy of marriage certificate. Waddington, New York.

John S. Rule, 81, of Waddington dies on Tuesday. (1928) *Commercial Advertiser.* Canton, New York.

Rule-Huntley. (1914). A very pretty home wedding. *The Madrid Harold.* Madrid, New York.

Scott, P. (2003) *The History of Strathbogie.* Tiverton, England: XL Publishing.

Scott, R. (1982) *Robert the Bruce.* Tiptree, Essex, England: Anchor Press Ltd.

Shaw, G. & Shaw, R. (1842-1900) *Tahawus-Newcomb and Long Lake.* Blue Mountain Lake, NY: Adirondack Experience.

Stoddard, R. (1874). Mitchell Sabattis of Long Lake. *The Adirondacks: Illustrated.* In a list by the proprietor of Long Lake Hotel, C .H. Kellogg .Retrieved, 2016. www.hamilton.nygenweb.net/bios/sabattis.html.

The Fair. St. Boswells Scotland. Retrieved January 26, 2017
http://www.stboswells.bordernet.co.uk/history/fair.html

Town of Chester. Town of Chester.org. Historical Society. Retrieved
December 2017. http://www.townofchesterny.org/

Town of Newcomb. Retrieved January 2018.
http://www.newcombny.com/about/history.

Willette, E. (2009) *The Girl from the Adirondack Mountains*. Xlibris
Corp. www.xlibris.com

Gail Huntley

OTHER SOURCES

I stayed in Scotland for a month with my sister and walked the highlands. We stayed in Huntly, and I spoke with librarians and authors of Scottish history. I saw many small farms, rivers, lochs, castles, and black-faced sheep dotting the hills. We stayed in a stone cottage much like where the Doddses lived but modernized.

I also visited many websites about the histories of the northern New York towns, such as Port Henry, Whitehall, and Crown Point and talked with librarians and historians in these towns.

Interviews with John and Phil Joseph about the Abenaki settlement near Saratoga Springs, New York, where their father's family lived.

Interviews with Jeff Rutherford about his connection to the Kellogg family and Lake Eaton, New York, where the Rutherfords settled in the book.

CPSIA information can be obtained
at www.ICGtesting.com
Printed in the USA
BVHW04s0749190818
524202BV00011B/15/P